I0620261

Tropical Spice

Sandy Loyd

DEDICATION

As always, this book is dedicated to my husband. But I also want to dedicate this book to my son and my sister. Without all of these people in my life, I would be lonelier and probably would never have come so far. I love you all.

OTHER BOOKS BY SANDY LOYD

Contemporary Romances

The California Series
Winter Interlude – Book One
Promises, Promises – Book Two
James – Book Three
Dancing With An Angel – Book Four

Second Chances Series
Tropical Spice – Book One
A Christmas Miracle – A Short Story

Romantic Suspense

D.C. Bad Boys Series
The Sin Factor – Book One
Raising the Stakes – Book Two

Running Series
Running From Love – Book One

Deadly Series
Deadly Misconceptions – Book One

A Matter of Trust

Kicker's Legacy

Chapter 1

Hunks who stepped over Second Chances' threshold normally didn't interest Pepper Grady. Not when the steady stream of hot-looking guys searching for a way to wind down after a day on the water never ended. Something about this one, as he strode through the bar with confidence evident in every step, drew her surreptitious gaze. A ray of light framed his face and highlighted strong aquiline features better than a Sharpie. And even more interesting? Every woman in the place noticed him. He was well aware of it. The sultry gleam emanating from those dark brown, soul-searing eyes told her so.

Okay. He was definitely worth a second glance, not to mention lots of ogling.

Second Chances wasn't exactly a *gin joint*—more like an upscale tourist hangout in the Florida Keys. Despite that, Pepper, a self-proclaimed classic movie aficionado, had a better appreciation for Humphrey Bogart's point of view when Ingrid walked into his life in *Casablanca*. Her attention stayed glued to the hunk as he sauntered further into the packed room even as the crowd seemed to part, allowing him space to navigate.

He gave the place a covert scan. When his focus landed her way, little tingles of awareness walked up her spine. Ignoring the sensation, Pepper sucked in a huge breath and wiped the bar in quick, easy motions in an effort to disengage from the stranger's pull.

He was only a male. One who probably expected women to bow at his feet…expected his charm and dynamite looks to pave the way to whatever he wanted, which Pepper figured amounted to a night in bed.

She grinned and gave the tall, well-toned mass of masculine perfection another stealthy once-over. The idea held merit. The minute the thought leapt out, Pepper discarded it. The guy looked too cocky. Besides, he had enough adulation without adding hers.

He'd clearly ranked at the top of his class in Seduction 101. No different than the thousands she'd seen in the three years she'd co-owned the bar. Of those thousands, more than half wore the same cap and gown of attitude…had graduated to the highest level. The stud level. All had the same moves, with all the same lines.

Pepper could recite most word for word. She'd heard them too many times. A sliver of regret slid over her at the idea that he'd be so unoriginal. *How disappointing.*

When he pulled out a stool not two feet away, she felt his gaze and her heartbeat quickened. The hairs on the back of her neck stood up. She didn't appreciate either reaction.

After a quick overview of the bar patrons and noting only full drinks, she turned her attention to washing glasses. Refills could wait, allowing a moment to reflect on the stranger's effect. Why did he cause such strong sensations? Was it pheromones? Some kind of magnetic attraction? Steeling herself, she glanced up, presenting her perfected bartender smile.

"What can I get you?" She was totally amazed at how calm her voice sounded despite how every nerve ending she possessed stood at full alert.

"What do you recommend?"

Mercy! Even his voice was sexy…exuding an arrogant maleness that said he conquered all women and took no prisoners. "Depends," she shot back, reaching for normal.

"Oh?"

"Yeah." Pepper's smile broadened, becoming more genuine. "Are you in the mood for a beer or would you like to experience a bit of the Keys?" She risked a quick glance at his eyes. Wrong thing to do. She refocused on a goblet and washed it for the third time.

"I think it's clean enough."

"What?" She looked up again and froze. A generous smile had taken over his face.

Ignore that smile. He's not charming. Do not let him get to you.

Point one went to the stranger, but a point was all she'd allow in his game. She straightened her spine and concentrated on rinsing the glass. In slow motion, she placed it on the strainer, before wiping her wet hands on her apron.

Her focus lifted, meeting his amused gaze. "I think you need Second Chances' specialty."

"Oh?" He hesitated a heartbeat. "I'm more interested in your specialty."

So sad and so expected. She'd heard *that* phrase just once too often.

Pepper flaunted a toothy grin, taking the point. "My specialty is shooting down guys like you without hurting egos. After all, I work for tips." She plunked the drink she'd hastily prepared in front of him, increased the wattage of her smile at the same time, and winked. "That'll be six dollars. Would you like to run a tab?"

Grin fading, he eyed her intently. Suddenly, another smile took his face, absolutely stealing her air, the punch of its effect landing with a hard thud against her chest.

"One will do." He pulled out his wallet and dropped a ten on the bar. "Keep the change. My *ego* is still intact."

Something in the way he said the words, a bit of Spanish inflection she hadn't heard earlier, caught her attention. Images of her father and older brother flashed through her mind. Then she rejected the notion. They had no clue as to her whereabouts. She'd hidden her past well. Angelina Delgado didn't exist in Marathon, Florida, gateway to some of the best sport fishing and scuba diving in the world. The key was miles away from the Caribbean island of her youth. Far from an overbearing *padré* determined to rule her life with his outdated notions. No one knew of Pepper Grady's auspicious beginnings. And she meant to keep it that way.

"Can I get another?"

She spun in the direction of the voice at the other end of the bar. "Coming right up." Pushing away thoughts of the stranger, she grabbed the lever, filled a chilled glass from the tap, then switched the full beer with the empty as she palmed the five the tourist held out.

With business brisk, she poured nonstop drinks as *he* slipped into the background. During a lull twenty minutes later, Pepper discreetly scanned the crowded bar noting, with not a little regret, he'd disappeared. She sighed. The stud was just another customer who tried to win her over and lost. Nothing more. Nothing less. For the rest of the night, she stayed too busy pouring drinks to worry over her reaction, much less think about it.

Eventually, the last customer finally left indicating the end of her shift. Damn, her feet hurt from standing on the bar's concrete floor for so long. Friday nights were always the busiest, meaning she usually worked from opening until closing. Thank goodness she only had one more hectic night before her vacation began. Then she'd have a week to do nothing but drive to Key West and hang out, or maybe head north to Miami for some shopping.

"Good night, Rach." Pepper nodded on her way out.

Co-owner Rachel Smith glanced up from her paperwork. "G'night."

Karen Black, the third partner and person in charge of the restaurant end of the bar, had left earlier, not long after the kitchen closed. Rachel handled details like withholding taxes and ordering because it was her strength. Pepper's was handling the customers. Their arrangement worked, affording the trio a lucrative lifestyle while living in paradise.

Pepper locked the door behind her. Rachel had a habit of working well past the one a.m. closing. Things were quiet on Grassy Key, given its location and Second Chances' high-end clientele this time of year, but why ask for trouble?

Late April meant weekends filled with South Floridians wanting a quick getaway, and vacationing hard-core divers or sport fishermen who left at the crack of dawn. All were usually ready for a drink and relaxation earlier than most vacationers, also ending their evenings earlier. Lack of sleep and too much alcohol could disrupt a diver's time underwater. And sport fishermen were more interested in their next day's catch than in being wild and crazy all night.

The minute the balmy night air hit her face, Pepper undid the scrunchie holding her thick black waist-length hair. Its heaviness fell like a mantle around her shoulders. Bending over, she rubbed her temples and pulled a hand through the lush tresses to allow the cooling effect the Atlantic Ocean's breeze provided. Long hair and tropical humidity didn't mix well, but Pepper couldn't bring herself to chop it off, dealing with its length and thickness as best she could. Someday she'd tire of having a furnace on her head. Until then, she'd persevere.

She straightened, surveyed the parking lot, and stopped abruptly, fingers still laced in her hair. Ignoring the little spark of pleasure spreading throughout her system, her elbow dropped. Then she ambled toward the dark shape perched against the hood of a sleek car, forgetting all about sore feet.

Pepper's stare remained steady, watching him watch her as she approached. His presence provided an element of excitement she hadn't felt in a long, long time, which only meant her life had become pretty damn boring. She halted a safe distance in front of him and crossed her arms. Whether a protective move or not, she wasn't sure.

"Fancy seeing you here." Her gaze took a trip over his gorgeous body, a twelve on a scale of one to ten. Though he sported the basic Keys wardrobe of shorts and a polo shirt—his were expensive and sheathed well-defined muscles like a glove.

"It's no accident," he said. "I'm waiting for you."

"Really?" She lifted her eyebrows and studied his masculine features, as she hadn't done earlier. Yep! Definitely Latin descent. The shadows magnified his dark hair and eyes. He probably lived in Miami. The slight inflection she caught again told her Spanish was his first language, most likely spoken at home. She'd heard the subtle nuances too often during her youth not to recognize his flawless English was a close second. Maybe his parents or grandparents were Cuban immigrants. Since Cuba was in the opposite direction of Isla del Diablo, she exhaled a sigh of relief.

"Yes, really." He grinned, the parking lot lights reflecting off straight white teeth. "It's huge."

When confusion clouded her eyes, a taunting midnight gaze seized and held hers.

"My ego, among other more important things," he clarified, still smiling.

She laughed, unable to hold back the burst of amusement. Point to the stranger, his taunts unexpected and refreshing. "Nice to know." Pepper turned to start off in the direction of her house, a short walk she made nightly, and said over her shoulder, "But

I'm not interested in egos or *other* things."

Attractive or not, everything about him shouted one-night stand and she was anything but. Though, surprisingly enough, she found herself tempted, which was why she opted for retreat.

"You're walking?" The incredulity in his loud voice disrupted the night sounds. The tree frogs and crickets quieted. An eerie silence trailed in the aftermath.

She pivoted, walking backward, and nodded. "Good deduction, I'm walking." As if on cue, the chorus began anew. She spun back around and continued, half-hoping he'd follow, if only to keep the game alive for a bit longer. She had to admit, he didn't bore her.

Within a moment, she felt his presence behind her. "I will escort you." The words were not a question, more like a command, nor did she miss the arrogance in them.

"Suit yourself." She shrugged, completely used to that Latino male superiority, one she'd encountered most of her life. "It's not far."

Sparing him a brief glimpse, she caught something in the firm line of his jaw.

Definitely a Hispanic male. His every ounce of masculinity conveyed the idea that she, a mere woman, couldn't manage on her own without his protection—a total misassumption.

Extensive tae kwan do training, along with the Monroe County Sheriff Department's defensive maneuvers course she'd taken after first setting foot in Florida, negated his false notion. Having been a pampered rich girl her entire life, she'd wanted to be able to defend herself in case the unthinkable happened. Single women without family nearby were easy targets. And Pepper decided long ago to be no man's easy target—even her father's—and certainly not this stranger's. She smiled inwardly. "I can take care of myself."

"A fact I have discovered firsthand."

She slanted another glance in his direction. The smug smile had returned.

Such a Spaniard! A hard one to ignore when he viewed her as if she were his next meal. Funny, how on other men that look was always enough to earn a quick put-down, but on him, it only made her wonder what would happen if…

"I do this for my own satisfaction. What kind of man would I be to let a beautiful woman walk the streets alone at this hour?"

What kind indeed, she thought, not replying and trying to ignore the companionable silence that had suddenly sprung up between them.

Neither spoke for nearly a quarter of a block before he asked, "Do my noble efforts gain me a name? Maybe some idle chitchat?"

Another laugh broke free. He'd earned another point. She'd best be careful, else he might win more than her name. This intriguing stranger had the uncanny ability to steal the game. She inhaled deeply, lightly biting her bottom lip, giving him a considering perusal.

"Pepper," she said, after a long moment and deciding she liked him. "Pepper Grady. Mr.…?"

"Nick Guerrero." He stuck out his hand.

"It's nice to meet you, Nick." She shook hands, noting a firm grip, also noting the way a spark of energy zapped life into her fingers. She swallowed hard, fighting stimulating sensations. "And what else do you hope your gallantry accomplishes?"

"That should be easy to deduce."

By this point, both had stopped walking. His smile, along with the amusement flashing from his eyes, almost lit the night sky. Yet she noted an unexpected sincerity in that gaze that was much more seductive. She tried to pull her hand away but his hold tightened, sending her heartbeat soaring. When he took her wrist to his mouth, she steeled her pulse to slow, praying he wouldn't notice how fast it zoomed.

"My lady's favor," he murmured, kissing that most sensitive spot just above her palm.

The heated tone in his voice spread over her like a warm blanket. And she wished his mouth wasn't so caressing…so moist…so inciting. In tandem, they ignited sparks. Uncontrolled pleasure shot everywhere. She shouldn't be aroused. Not with such a lame line and a smooth move, but she had to admit, they did the trick.

Now she understood why others succumbed to the exquisite

torment. One consisting of a combination of timing, attraction, pheromones, and who knew what else, that went into the perfect seduction. She darn sure didn't think conditions got more perfect than this. Pepper had never felt this free, this alive, or this needy. Not like he made her feel at the exact moment she'd finally yanked her fingers from his grasp.

Alarm bells pealed in her brain. This man was dangerous.

For the first time in Pepper's life, she could see herself in the throes of passion. With Nick. Very disturbing, given she'd just met him and knew nothing about him. Though many had tried, no man had ever wielded such influence after only a short walk and a few words.

Secretly, she observed him, searching for some clue as to why him. Why now?

In an instant of insight, the truth hit. He epitomized men of power and wealth, men she'd sworn off, men like her father and her brother. The same supreme confidence the Delgado men exuded was stamped into every nuance of his body.

Pepper stiffened. Her pulse quickened. Only this time, the cause was wariness over his nearness, not excitement.

Walk. Just keep walking. Adhering to her mental commands, she forced movement, put one foot in front of the other.

He followed, strolling silently beside her. *Of course he would. He had to sense he was close to his prize. A hunting tiger aware of his tiring prey.*

The closer they got to her house, the more wary she became, even regretting her impulse to allow his escort. Oh, she wasn't afraid of him in the sense that he might harm her. This fear went deeper because he'd somehow snuck in under her guard.

Looking straight ahead, her mind spun as more similarities surfaced. Oh, yes. The signs were there. Hadn't she escaped her father's heavy hand and become who she wanted to be...her own woman? She'd come too far to let a man like Nick Guerrero waltz into her life and begin controlling.

She'd survived thus far without having passion in her life. Passion was overrated anyway, made heartbroken fools of women. Her mother's life, a prime example, was one Pepper had no intention of replicating. Ever.

~

Angelina, or Pepper, as she called herself, stopped at the edge of a walkway leading to a cozy bungalow that rose well above the ground on a foundation of stilts. A burst of pride shot through Nico Fernández considering the location. She wasn't hurting financially. Though not huge, the ocean view meant the charming house had to be worth a tidy sum. Her mother's trust fund helped to buy the bar, but he knew firsthand Pepper Grady bought the house from her own earnings, not family money. For some reason, the fact pleased him.

"Well, Nick. I appreciate the escort. But I think I can handle it from here." She gave him a curt nod of dismissal before turning and walking purposefully toward the house.

"I disagree." Nico grinned, not about to be brushed off like a piece of lint from fine velvet. "A gentleman makes sure his lady's premises are secure."

She halted in midstep, then turned to face him with shoulders squared. "I'm not *your lady*, so that won't be necessary."

A mere technicality he planned to change. "Seems we're at an impasse." When he caught the hint of irritation flare in those expressive amber eyes, his grin stretched. "Surely you wouldn't withhold the opportunity of proving myself a true gentleman?"

Her quick laugh traveled through his ears straight to his gut with the force of liquid fire.

Angelina had been a total surprise. No, not Angelina. Until he was ready to make his true identity known, he'd have to think of her as Pepper, and he had to remain Nick Guerrero, not Antonio "Nico" Fernández, the name she'd recognize, keeping to his *madré's* maiden name and an Americanized form of his nickname.

"Good night, Nick," she said, once her laughter died. She offered a negligent salute and started walking. "Thanks for the company. I haven't laughed so hard in ages."

El cielo me ayuda. Heaven help him. He certainly needed divine intervention to restrain the strong urge to kiss that mocking mouth and show her exactly how gentlemanly he was being by allowing her to walk away. "*Hasta la vista, querida*," Nico murmured, watching her slow retreat.

Miguel Delgado had warned him to tread carefully around his youngest daughter. After all, she'd disappeared without a clue from Isla del Diablo and it had taken the elder Delgado an entire year to track her down. It was Ñico's job to return her to where she belonged.

The moment she closed her door with a final click, he turned, retracing the path they'd come. Anticipation strummed through his blood as thoughts of the task ahead filled his brain. She'd had a couple of years of freedom, but duty now called. It was time for her to honor her father's wishes. Isla del Diablo needed her. Ñico needed her cooperation and he would have it. He would also have her; he'd decided the moment he laid eyes on her.

Her earlier put-downs told him she'd be a challenge, giving him the niggling feeling that not many had breached her prickly exterior. This idea delighted him. Immensely. He held no doubts about succeeding where others had failed. The attraction was there. He saw it in her eyes, in her body's response to his signals. She was no more immune to him than he was to her. One thing he knew was how to please a woman, make her yearn for his touch.

Ñico gave a quick glance over his shoulder. "*Sí, mi ángel pequeña*, Pepper," he said, just before he lost sight of her house. His little angel would soon be his, in both name and body.

~

Once safely hidden from Nick Guerrero's penetrating gaze, Pepper leaned her head against the door frame, stilling the compulsion to run after him and drag him back inside.

What was wrong with her? It had taken every bit of her willpower not to yield to his sexy smile. She'd come so close to agreeing to his tempting offer to check her premises. Pepper had no illusions about a man like him. If he ever made it through her front door, he might figure a way around her renewed defenses.

She hated to admit that the overbearing, supremely male attitude he had going held a strong appeal. Mercy. How could that be? She'd never thought she'd be a sucker for a man who reminded her of her father.

Maybe she was her mother's daughter after all. A sobering thought.

Pepper sighed and started for the kitchen. Nick Guerrero held too many similarities to the men she'd spent a great deal of effort avoiding. The memory of the bleak unhappiness and pain reflected in her mother's eyes was reminder enough to hold on to her resolve of not falling for a man like her father. She'd be a fool to allow a man such as Nick into her life. Problem was, she couldn't totally dismiss the idea of having a torrid affair with him—a very disturbing thought. Had her life really become so unexciting? Unfortunately, the truth of that question was a sad yes.

Pepper grabbed a couple of brownies and headed for her patio overlooking the ocean. A balmy breeze carrying the scent of the ocean wafted through strands of her hair and tickled her nose. For a long time she sat staring at the calming dark water, eating and contemplating her options.

She wasn't exactly the "love 'em and leave 'em" type. She'd steered clear of men in general, an easy feat on Isla del Diablo given an overprotective father and brother. No available male had dared venture near her. Even in college, they'd been scarce thanks to her brother.

Too bad her standards were so high once she'd made her escape. No one had caught her fancy in the last four years. She didn't consider herself a prude…truthfully never thought she'd be well into her twenties without having had at least a few lovers. Yet, older and wiser, she couldn't help being pickier. She certainly hadn't succumbed to *love* like her mother had. None of those who'd filed through the bar with their disappointing lines made her heart go pitter-patter. Not like Nick.

She bit into a brownie and smiled, wondering what would happen if she played his game. The more she thought about the intriguing man, the more she liked the idea, but she'd have to twist the game and play it her way. She had no intention of losing her heart to someone like him. She'd win his instead.

Chapter 2

After a quick workout at the gym the next morning, Pepper turned onto her street and spied Nick sitting on her top step. She parked, climbed out of the car, and ambled toward him, not bothered by the already hot Florida sun beating against her back, heating up the thick mass of dark hair pulled up haphazardly on her head, still slightly damp from a shower. She loved the heat. Loved the humidity. Both reminded her of home.

Eyeing the suntanned hunk thoughtfully, Pepper halted a few feet from him. "Fancy seeing you here." She quelled the thrill of excitement running through her, thankful she had only a little time before she needed to leave for work. Otherwise, she might be tempted to invite him inside, not a good idea.

He grinned. "It's no accident," he said, playing along with her words of last night. "I'm waiting for you." He lifted a holder with two large cups of coffee. "It's not Cuban, but it's strong."

A smile tugged at the edges of her mouth, working to break free. The man had certainly guessed one of her weak spots. "Thanks." Pepper grasped the cup he held out, ignoring the small twinge the contact caused when her hand brushed his. "I shouldn't tell you this, but strong coffee after a workout will get you much more than my name and idle conversation."

"So I was hoping."

She sat next to him, keeping a safe space in between. "Exactly what else were you hoping for?"

"A chance to get to know you."

"That's it?"

Nick shrugged. "My intentions include getting to know you...*thoroughly*."

There they were. That sexy voice accompanied with that sizzling, thousand-degree stare. Both sent goose bumps up her arms, despite the sun's warmth. She grinned, then placed her coffee aside and stood. It was time to change the rules of the game and show him she was no pushover. Leaning over, she grazed his lips, holding his rapt attention.

"I'm offering fair warning. I'm not an easy person to get to know."

He had such inviting lips. She gave in to temptation—after all, why play if she couldn't take chances—and lowered her mouth the last quarter inch. Pepper spent a long moment enjoying the liquid sensation of pleasure flowing through every vein the contact provided.

Boy, did he know how to use that mouth.

Before she lost herself in kissing Nick, she pulled away, but was hampered with a vice-like grip on her arm. He tugged her off balance and she landed on his lap. Seconds later, he smothered her protests with the hottest kiss she'd ever tasted while his hands stroked slowly up and down her back.

Instantly, Pepper regretted her hasty taunting as a blast of heat engulfed her when she felt his arousal underneath her bottom. She fought the yearning building, unwilling to let him know how much his actions affected her, because she sensed women were always succumbing to that mouth. It was too early in this crazy game to afford him so much leverage. Otherwise, she'd end up the loser. Using every ounce of self-preservation she owned, she broke the kiss.

This time, he let her rise.

"Like I said. I'm not easy," she was able to get out with some modicum of control, meeting Nick's fiery gaze. "Thanks for the coffee." Then, ignoring those hot, soul-searing eyes, she picked up her cup and strode into her house without a backward glance.

~

Nico stared at the door she'd disappeared behind while taking several deep breaths, expelling the air slower after each one. He stifled the strong impulse to follow and brought his coffee to his lips for a long drink, considering his next step. Still eyeing the door, a grin snuck up on him. His heiress had certainly thrown down the verbal gauntlet.

He hadn't realized until now how much he might relish the challenge.

"*Dios*," he murmured, rolling his eyes skyward praying for help. It was a damn necessity to restrain his dual desires—the desire to throttle her and the desire to kiss that smart mouth until she was crying out her release. How could the goddess he'd held in his arms, a goddess who kissed like an angel, be the same taunting wildcat who evoked a strong urge to subdue her?

A novel and humbling experience, to be sure. Ñico couldn't remember a time he'd had to subdue any woman into submitting to his kisses. Not ever. Not when women were always available. Yet, instinct told him he couldn't rush things with Pepper or he'd never get what he wanted.

And what exactly was that? Far more than one night, that was for damn sure.

The thought-provoking question and answer brought him up short.

Ñico stood to leave, not liking the direction his thoughts traveled. In less than twelve hours, his heiress had succeeded in driving him to the brink of distraction. He'd barely slept. The anticipation of seeing her again had kept him awake for hours, another unusual occurrence. Ordinarily, he didn't worry about attaining a woman's attention. Whether for a week, his shortest, or a few months, his longest, most relationships just fell into place for him with very little effort or worry on his part. He was quickly realizing Pepper wouldn't be so accommodating, and patience wasn't one of his virtues.

He didn't like the suspended state of arousal mere thoughts of her evoked.

He snorted and climbed inside his rental, refusing to believe she had any sway over his thoughts. Pepper was only a woman, and no matter how beautiful, Ñico wasn't about to let her affect him any more than she already had. This was lust, something he could control.

He started the car and backed up. Since it had been awhile, he'd just have to rectify the situation. Soon.

~

"Hey, Karen," Pepper said forty-five minutes later, strolling into Second Chances. Morning sunshine filtered through a wall of windows opening to the ocean's view and illuminated the main dining room, spotlighting the tidy and shiny surfaces. Pepper, along with Karen and Rachel, had slaved long hours to create an inviting atmosphere with profitable results.

"Hey, Pep." Karen glanced up from the big soup pot and stopped stirring.

The kitchen door was propped open, giving both women the opportunity to talk while they did their morning prep work.

Humming, Pepper stepped behind the mahogany bar, an antique they'd picked up at an auction, and grabbed an apron, tying it around her middle. This morning she'd woken up energized, and felt even more so now, bolstered no doubt from kissing Nick. After such a great beginning to her day, she was totally prepared for the hours ahead. She'd most likely be able to take a long break in between the lunch lull and the dinner hour. "What's today's special?"

"Conch chowder and grouper." Karen smiled, then went back to stirring. "Big John had a good day yesterday," she said of one of their sources, locally known for the freshest catches on the island.

"I'm glad." Big John, a nickname he earned because the brawny man was well over six feet five inches, always made sure Karen and Second Chances had the best pick.

"Thank God for attraction," Pepper murmured. Attraction had its uses. She'd noted the way Big John's eyes never left her friend whenever they shopped in his fish market together. His crush aided in Second Chances' reputation for fresh seafood at reasonable prices. He wasn't the only vendor to do so. The locals treated the three owners like celebrities. A trio of attractive women running a successful bar and restaurant was a bit of a novelty in this part of the Keys. The three friends never flaunted or abused their looks or their status, nor did they keep from graciously accepting the little extras because of them.

"I'm only making half a pot. I don't anticipate a hectic day."

Pepper nodded and began readying the bar. The weather didn't dictate the seasons. Tourists did. With the spring breaks over and the snowbirds flying back to their summer nests, her piece of paradise was left emptier. The action at the bar would be nil until later this afternoon. Fridays and Saturdays were the only days she and Karen handled the midday crowds together. Soon, they'd split those days between them until it picked up again.

Months ago, Rachel had talked them into hiring an assistant

manager, which cut into their take-home pay. But Rachel had a valid point with her biggest argument. What good was money if you didn't have time to enjoy it?

"What'd you think of the hunk last night?" Karen strode up to her with two bowls of soup. She placed them in front of her, perched on a stool, and pushed one toward Pepper.

"Hunk?" She snuffed a rising flame of annoyance. Karen had to be referring to Nick. Second Chances' chef had a thing for any tall, dark, and sexy man, and Pepper considered Nick hers. At least till he no longer interested her, which might be awhile.

"Like you didn't see him?" Karen grinned, shaking her head. "I've got eyes. And they didn't miss what either of yours did. His followed your every move until he left."

"Okay, so I noticed." Pepper picked up the spoon and began eating, hoping Karen would drop it. For some reason, she felt funny discussing her real thoughts about what she planned to do with Nick. Mercy, maybe she was a prude!

"You'll see him again. My money says he'll be in today."
Pepper swallowed a spoonful of soup, then cleared her throat. "He walked me home last night, then was waiting on my front porch with a cup of coffee when I got back from the gym this morning." A streak of heat rose along her face. Why should it embarrass her to mention his visit?

"Oh my God!" Karen's spoon dropped with a plop into her bowl, her mouth making the perfect O as her eyes widened. "He walked you home? Are you crazy? How could you let a perrfect stranger know where you live?"

Pepper shrugged. Crazy wasn't far off the mark.
Karen waited a beat and then prodded, "It's obvious you survived. But answer me this, why are you so coolly slurping soup, when *he* brought you coffee? I'd be peeing in my pants."

Pepper kept her focus on eating and didn't respond, unwilling to reveal how apt her description seemed. She could barely contain her excitement.

A moment later, she felt Karen's gaze. She glanced up, noting her friend's sobered expression.

"Boy, are you a fraud. You almost fooled me." With a narrowed gaze, Karen snorted. "You're not as cool as I thought, are you?"

"What can I say?" Pepper shrugged. "He *is* a hunk. A hunk who's impossible not to notice, especially when he shows up unexpectedly."

"It's about damn time." She tsk-tsked, returning her attention to her bowl of soup. "It's unnatural. You're a beautiful woman in the prime of life, yet you might as well be an old lady the way you keep guys at a distance. I only hope he succeeds in putting some fun into your life. If anyone needs it, you do."

"I have fun. Aren't I taking a vacation?"

Karen offered a skeptical grunt. "First one in three years?"

"Oh, like you're so frivolous? You never take any time either."

"But I use my days off during the week in a more recreational way. What do you do besides go home to watch old movies or work with dolphins?"

"They're entertaining pastimes. Much more than most of the guys who're always ready with some stupid line."

"How do you know? You never give any guy a chance, blowing him off before he even gets a few sentences out."

"I do not." Pepper's back stiffened. She swallowed the last bit of chowder, and pushed the empty bowl forward. She shouldn't have to defend herself. If she wasn't interested, she wasn't interested.

"Yes. You do." Rolling her eyes, Karen took another bite. Then using her spoon to emphasize her words, she aimed it at her. "Such a sad way to live, Pep. You need to lighten up. In case you haven't noticed, Humphrey Bogart is dead…has been since the late fifties. And your hunk is alive and kicking. What's more, he brought you coffee."

"I see your point." Pepper sighed heavily.

Lately she'd become disinterested in just about everything, barely had the energy to watch even Bogie. Nick's arrival couldn't be timed better. He seemed the perfect solution to her apathy. The thought brought her up short. Okay, maybe Karen's words held more than a bit of truth. Hadn't she been lamenting to herself just days ago she felt something missing? Contrary to what Karen said, she loved her romantic old movies. Only they just weren't enough any longer.

After giving so much time and energy in the past few years to

17

Second Chances, she needed a change. Since Geri McGuire, their newly hired assistant, was easing some of their load, Pepper suddenly decided she looked forward to taking her earned time off.

Karen went back to eating while Pepper grabbed the bottle of gin she'd opened right before Karen had interrupted with soup. She secured a pouring spout on top, then set it with the other liquor bottles lining the back wall.

The more she thought about Nick, the more her decision solidified. It *was* time for fun. Another eye-opener. Still, she wasn't exactly willing to attribute her melancholy mood to the opposite sex, or lack of having someone in her life. But she had to admit, Nick's presence did provide a sense of anticipation she hadn't experienced in years. His dark good looks and gorgeous body were an added bonus, too hard to resist for any healthy twenty-five-year-old woman. The hot Latino male she'd found sitting on her step earlier promised excitement, if nothing else.

~

"There you go, Bob," Pepper said two hours later. She placed his order in front of him. Her one other regular customer at the opposite end of the bar had already received his lunch.

Slow didn't begin to describe the hour they'd been open. Pepper used the opportunity to train their new assistant how to tend bar. Geri, perfect assistant manager material, liked all aspects of Second Chances and absorbed every word Pepper uttered better than a sponge.

Besides teaching the basics of making mai tais, Pepper took a physical inventory. Geri watched and recorded every step into her little notebook. Though they had a program tied into Second Chances' register that estimated usage based on sales, Pepper still had to reconcile any differences several times a year. At least now the task wouldn't be waiting when she returned from vacation. Pepper hated paperwork and usually spent more time creating excuses to avoid it. But today for some reason, she'd found she needed to stay mentally busy. So she wouldn't think of *him*.

The *him* she'd been diligently avoiding in her mind stepped inside just then, drawing her gaze. Damn, he looked good.
Like last night, he nonchalantly scanned the room before his focus landed on her.

Instantly, warmth stole up her face. Pepper's heartbeat raced as he sauntered toward the bar, authority and arrogance apparent in every step, his chocolate gaze still zeroed in on her.

She tamped down her excitement and wiped the bar she'd already thoroughly cleaned, refusing to let the guy affect her any further. She'd go at her own pace, not his. Unfortunately, her body wasn't into listening to her mind's commands.

"What can I get you, *stranger*?" Her usual bartender smile disappeared behind a genuine one when she made eye contact.

Nick's grin was quick. "Second Chances' specialty, of course." Grabbing a stool, he sat with a casual confidence, then winked. "I'd love to taste *your* specialty again, but somehow I doubt it's on the menu."

Pepper chuckled. Preparing the drink, she fought to think of a quick comeback. Darn, if Nick didn't earn another point with that comment, and yet another because his heated eyes were still making it next to impossible to keep a coherent thought in her head.

She placed the drink in front of him. But she wasn't fast enough. In an unexpected move, he'd covered her hand with his. The contact sent a jolt of pleasure straight to her midsection. Besides warmth, she also felt strength in his fingers. She forced herself to keep breathing, trying hard to act as if his touch didn't cause the earth to move.

"May I have my hand back?" Pepper raised her chin as well as her eyebrows, eyeing him more warily, feeling like a small animal caught in a trap. "Please?" she whispered, hoping she really didn't sound so pathetic.

"For a price."

"Oh?" She swallowed hard. Mercy, she'd pay anything to keep Nick's hand right where it was, but somehow she knew it wasn't in her best interest. "And what would that be?" she was able to ask without disgracing herself too much.

"A little bit of your time."

"My time?" Ignoring the tingles of pleasure his thumb set off as he rubbed it lightly over her wrist, she worked to keep from promising him more than time. Using more force, she yanked.

He let her hand go and his grin spread. "Surely you get a break? Maybe I can take you to lunch or something."

Pepper laughed after returning to some semblance of control. "I've already had lunch."

Unfortunately, Karen chose that moment to barge through the kitchen door. She stopped short when she spied Nick and ran her gaze over his body with a quick up-and-down motion of her head. Her smile held a bit of speculation.

"So the hunk returns," she said, giving Pepper an I-told-you-so look.

"I'm Nick Guerrero." He held out his hand.

"Karen Black, Mr. Guerrero," Karen murmured, taking it. "Nick."

Pepper tamped down the surge of annoyance over Karen's flirting. Did she have to be so stunning? So petite? So blue-eyed and blonde, the complete opposite of her? She didn't have a petite bone in her body, and her dark brunette looks seemed too stark and shadowy, like night against day, almost dull next to such perkiness.

Nick dropped her hand and nodded toward Pepper. "I was hoping to entice Pepper away for a quick bite."

"That's perfect." Karen slid behind the bar and started undoing her apron. "The bar's dead right now. In fact, take the night off. Geri's ready to cover for you."

At the moment their assistant was out of the bar running an errand.

"I'm still training her," Pepper said, chickening out all of a sudden, not sure if she could handle being alone with Nick for too long without self-combusting. Her emotions were volatile right now. If she needed more proof, all she had to do was look into those dark, electric eyes.

"Use another excuse," Karen said, seeing right through her tactics and handing over her apron. "She'll be fine. And Rach and I'll be here just in case."

"Who'll be fine?" Rachel asked, breezing through the same door Karen had. She also halted in midstride. With much interest, her gaze took a swift trip over Nick's body. Then Rachel's attention shifted, seeking Pepper's. Her eyebrows rose, clearly asking, *Who's the hunk?*

"Another beautiful woman." Nick's smile broadened. "So many in one room is a treat." He smiled and held out his hand again. "I'm Nick."

Pepper bit her tongue, wishing both partners could simply disappear. Not liking where her thoughts were going, she answered Rachel's question once the introductions were over. "Geri." She cleared her throat. "Nick asked me out this afternoon." She shrugged. "I'm not sure Geri can handle the bar alone just yet."

"Karen's right. She'll be fine." Rachel brushed her concern away with a wave of the same hand Nick had released. "If it gets too busy, I'm here."

Nick glanced at her, his smile gloating that he'd overcome the obstacle she'd thrown out. "Apparently, your partners have freed you from your duties."

"Okay," she agreed lamely, having no other alternative. "Geri can work for a couple of hours and I'll come in later to check on her. Make sure she can handle things," she added, leaving herself with an out. She certainly didn't want to be rushed with such a drastic step, nor did she want to roll over and accept his bidding, like a trained dog. In order to win this game, she needed to ease into sex. Somehow, given the electricity sizzling in the air their attraction generated, easing might not be an option. Not if he got her completely alone and she had no backup plan.

They walked out of Second Chances.

"Now that you have my undivided attention for a few hours, what are we going to do?" Pepper rolled her eyes, mentally kicking herself. Why not just hand him an extra point with such an inane statement.

"You're a local," Nick said, obviously taking pity on her. By letting the comment slide, he earned the point anyway, which concerned her more than if he'd made some snide innuendo. *And that's exactly why he's so dangerous.* "What do you suggest?"

Pepper shrugged and viewed him through a narrow-eyed gaze. "Most people come to the Keys for the fishing or the diving."

"Do you dive?"

"I'm certified." His eyebrows shot up and she smiled. Her news definitely surprised him. "How about you?" When Nick nodded, she added, "Sombrero Reef is about five miles straight out that way." She pointed toward the blue waters of the Atlantic.

"The underwater sanctuary is part of the only natural reef in North America. It's worth the time, but we really need an earlier start to do it right."

"How about tomorrow?" He grinned. "That is, if you can spare the time to *do it right?*"

"I don't have a boat," she objected, shaking her head. Damn if he didn't know exactly how to use his innuendos, not wasting them on lame topics.

"No problem. I'll rent one." Nick picked up her hand and raised it to his mouth, catching her gaze with his before he pressed his lips to that sensitive spot on the underside of her wrist, providing exquisite torture as her heart skipped beats.

"How about it, *querida?* Will you sail and dive with me tomorrow?"

When he called her sweetheart like that, his hot voice sending shivers down her spine and those sultry eyes searing her soul, she'd darn well follow him anywhere. *So this is what it's like to be seduced.*

She smiled, enjoying the sensations of warmth spreading. *Remember, Pepper, it's only a game. Maybe,* she mentally argued with herself, *but it's a damn fun one.* If she'd known how thrilling it felt to be seduced, she might have given one of those other men Karen had mentioned a shot.

"Sailing and diving sound like the perfect way to start a vacation." Along with a little seduction, it sounded the perfect way to have even more fun. Her grin widened. "But that doesn't solve our immediate problem."

"Hmmm, you're right." Nick stroked his chin, giving the matter some thought. "How about local sightseeing? I hear there is plenty to see. Let's start with the Dolphin Research Center."

"Sure, why not."

"Good." He pointed to a parked Mercedes. "We can take my car if you navigate."

His hand landed at the small of her back and as he guided her in that direction, Pepper worked at remaining calm. The sudden awareness of his nearness had her doubting her ability to keep things from happening too fast. At least they'd be around other tourists who'd provide company as well as some protection, so Pepper could catch her breath and think. Nick Guerrero had a way about him that kept her from doing both.

~

Ñico led Pepper to his car and surreptitiously studied her. Such a goddess, a Spanish queen, who deigned walk beside an underling. That's what he saw in the straight line of her back, in the tilt of her head, in the grace of her gait. He sensed a skittishness about her, yet she was enticing at the same time. An interesting dichotomy and very arousing to a man like him, one who tired quickly of the game, especially when the women he usually came into contact with were as skilled as he and looked at him as prey to be taken down.

The thought stopped him. When had he become so cynical? Wealth and power brought out the vultures and they were always circling. It was refreshing to see not a vulture, but a swan in the woman striding beside him.

Pepper definitely wasn't used to the "fast lane" those in his circle traveled. Though he deemed her savvy and sophisticated given their earlier run-ins, he hadn't missed the hint of embarrassment his earlier play produced. She seemed much more comfortable fielding repartee than exploiting it for flirting.

"Is something wrong?" she asked a moment later.

"Wrong?" Ñico glanced at her with a furrowed brow.

She shrugged. "You seem quiet all of a sudden."

"What could be wrong? I'm in a beautiful spot with a beautiful woman who has bestowed a beautiful gift. Her time. I'm simply glad you have given me this opportunity to get to know you."

By this time, they'd reached the car. He opened her door.

"Flattery will get you far, you know."

He chuckled softly. "All part of the plan." She climbed inside and he hurried to join her. With his seat belt fastened, he gave her a considering glance. "So, tell me about Pepper Grady."

"What would you like to know?" she asked, as he pulled onto the main highway.

"Everything."

"That's too broad. I don't even think I know everything."

"Ah. Now you're being evasive. Should I worry? Are there skeletons in your closet? Another man to consider?"

Pepper flashed him a secret smile, enchanting him further.

Dios! He didn't want to take his eyes off those kissable lips, but he had to drive. He refocused on the road ahead and prayed he could stick to his resolve to proceed slowly. This need her nearness caused was hard to ignore and was eating a hole in his gut.

"Well?" he asked.

"Well what?"

"I'm waiting for your answer."

"Oh." She shook her head. "No skeletons here. And it's just me. No one else to consider."

When she remained steadfastly mute during the next two miles, Ñico chuckled. "I see I'm to ask specific questions if I'm to learn anything."

"Sorry." She giggled, the sound captivating him even more, if that were possible. "I'm not very good at talking about myself."

"Ah. The perfect woman."

"Hardly."

He scanned the length of her body, grinning. "Pretty damn near perfect from my vantage point."

Pepper blushed, the pink stealing quickly across her cheekbones. *Dios,* he hadn't had seen a woman blush in much too long and the idea that he was the cause was intoxicatingly sexy.

Again, she remained silent.

"What do you like to do in your spare time?" he asked, in an attempt to get her talking about herself. He wasn't quite sure why, but at this moment, his curiosity stirred.

"You don't want to know." She hesitated. "I'm sure someone like you will find the information boring."

"Try me."

Ñico kept his smile warm as she eyed him warily. "Okay. Don't say I didn't warn you." She flashed a ready grin. "I'm an old movie buff."

"Old movies?" His eyes grew the size of quarters.

"Yes, preferably those before the 1960s."

His grin expanded. "You mean like *Casablanca* and *Vertigo*?"

"Yes." Pepper offered a slow nod, still smiling. "They're classics."

"I know." He nodded. "And two of my favorites."

"Mine too," she gushed. Suddenly more words burst forth, tumbling out of her mouth without reserve about the classic movies she adored. Her enthusiasm came through loud and clear.

"So another favorite is *Gone With The Wind*?" he asked, surprised at the revelation as she started to wind down.

"Yes."

Ñico sucked in a deep breath, as another one of her smiles taunted him. This feeling of pleasure grew from within and wasn't sexual. Who knew they shared such a similar love of entertainment? There was obviously much more to the woman he intended to marry than what met the eye. He meant to uncover *everything* about her. "So, tell me. What do you like better? The love story or its depiction of one of the most turbulent eras of United States' history?"

"Neither."

"Neither?" He turned into the center's parking lot and parked. Switching off the ignition, he twisted in the seat with the question in his eyes. "Explain yourself."

"Clark Gable. Need I say more?"

"Usurped by a dead man?" He put his hand to his chest, mocking dismay. But he couldn't halt the smile from taking over his face.

"Not just any dead man. He's a legend. Although I've read he had false teeth and Vivian Leigh hated kissing him in that movie." Pepper bit her lower lip, suppressing a grin. "I refuse to believe ugly rumors, nor will I allow the presence he depicted on the silver screen to be so depressingly erased with such nonsense, which is why I've never researched the truth. I prefer my fantasies. And I also prefer to utilize my imagination as to whether they got back together. I never liked the sequel."

"There was a sequel?"

"Alexandra Ripley's version. You didn't read it?"

Ñico shrugged, rolling his eyes. "I missed it." His answer drew her soft laugh, the musical lilt wrapping around his ears. *Dios*, he loved her laugh.

"I've mentally written my own version."

His eyebrows rose, drawing another laugh. Such a sweet sound, one he decided fit the woman. He had no interest in Gable or this Ripley, but he could listen to her laughter all day. A thought struck, hitting him with the jarring force of a bucket of ice water. Angelina Delgado, or Pepper Grady, whatever she went by, was a woman he wanted to possess. He eyed her intently. Why? A burning question to be sure, but why did he feel so comfortable with her that he could discuss something as ridiculous as old movies and why did she draw out this sudden need?

"I rather like the idea of both mellowing with time and still finding passion in their old age." Pepper winked, saying conspiratorially, "That's the beauty of Mitchell's ending. It's left up to the reader as to what happens later, especially since she's dead and we'll never know hers."

"I see." Ñico's eyes focused on her kissable lips, as the words filtering past his brain didn't register.

She snorted. "No, you don't. But that's okay."

She pulled the handle and opened the door, yanking him out of his musings.

He stepped out of the car and hurried to her side.

"I have a more pragmatic view of the ending." Then he said, more to see her reaction than give a point of view, "Scarlett blew it with Rhett."

Pepper's brow furrowed. A gust of wind caught her hair, blowing it. She reached to push it out of her eyes. With elbow up, stilling errant strands, her gaze ran over his body. "I wouldn't take you for a cynic." She sighed and shook her head. "But then I never took you for a person who'd visit dolphins in his spare time, either." She turned a full circle in the parking lot, looking much like a long-haired young Mary Tyler Moore hitting Minneapolis in those Nick at Nite oldies he also enjoyed watching. She grinned. "I love this place." She waited a heartbeat and added, "So, who are you, Nick Guerrero?"

"What you see before you is what you get." He held out his hands palms up. "A mere man who finds you attractive." He glanced at the building she pointed to. The Dolphin Research Center. The facility was renowned with a far-reaching reputation. She needn't know that tracking and seducing one missing heiress wasn't his only purpose for this trip. "And a man who likes dolphins."

She headed for the entrance. Ñico followed, fully intending to check it out and see what he could exploit as far as research went for a similar facility he chaired on Isla del Diablo. The fact that his time with Pepper aided in this endeavor was a plus. A very definite plus.

"You're not what I expected." She stopped and waited till he caught up with her.

He stayed silent, his thoughts mirroring her words. The lady was nothing close to what he expected. Though her regal bearing reminded him of Spanish royalty, she was nothing like the spoiled princess he'd expected, the same one who'd run away from her duty in a fit of temper four years ago.

"You like dolphins?"

"Yes." He ignored her skeptical expression and turned to hit the keyless lock on his rental. He slanted a glance at her before reaching for the building's door handle, and grinned. "What? You doubt I could find sea life fascinating?" Ñico understood the fine balance of nature and progress. Without the natural resources of the Caribbean, his island's inhabitants wouldn't be as prosperous.

"No." Pepper heaved a lengthy sigh and eyed him carefully. "I didn't realize we had something else in common."

"Oh?"

She shrugged and slid through the door he held open. "Contrary to my partners' opinion, I do have some semblance of a life." She looked over her shoulder and the smile she bestowed hit him like a battering ram to the gut. "I don't watch movies all the time. I volunteer here on my days off."

He nodded. Another hidden dimension to his heiress. He'd determined to enjoy the chase and savor a physical relationship for as long as it lasted. Yet he was beginning to admire her, something of a novelty with the women he usually dated. He couldn't name one woman he'd been intimate with in the last year he actually admired. He found them attractive, stunning even, good conversationalists who knew how to work a party, but not much else.

He shook the sobering thoughts, unwilling to dissect his love life, and followed her inside.

She turned. "Are you ready for a treat?" Her voice held laughter.

A long-forgotten memory surfaced and Ñico was suddenly fifteen again, standing at the edge of the blue-green Caribbean, as this young, exuberant vision came splashing out of the sea, running at top speed toward him. Then she plopped onto the sand in front of him and asked him to wait for her to grow up. He'd thought her crush amusing and readily agreed to her silly request, but he also remembered feeling an ethereal connection to this little sea nymph, which was the true reason he hadn't been able to disappoint her with a *no*. So long ago, yet the image of that connection was vivid, as if it had happened yesterday. And even more disturbing? The same sense of connection with her overwhelmed him now.

The impish smile Pepper wore had brought more memories to mind. Though he hadn't seen her in person since that summer day, he'd seen pictures and had received his father's updates on her life on Isla del Diablo. No one had coerced him into the arranged marriage his father had demanded on his twenty-fifth birthday, five years earlier. At that time, it seemed a perfect alliance. His eagerness had diminished entirely once he discovered her desertion a year later, just days before they were to meet again as adults. As far as Ñico was concerned, life was too short to be tied to a woman who'd disdained the thought of marriage to him so much she'd run away without even giving him the courtesy of an explanation. Back then, he'd fought unsuccessfully to be released from his original promise—realizing it for what it was—a stupid, useless effort to earn his *padré's* attention and one he'd bitterly regretted because it hadn't worked.

Unfortunately, circumstances had a way of muddying his emotional waters and causing him to reconsider his arranged marriage. His father had myelofibrosis, a form of bone marrow cancer, manageable for years with diet, exercise, and low doses of chemo, but the disease heralded his mortality. Traditions remained strong on his native island located at the edge of the Caribbean Sea, not far from Puerto Rico. Though Ñico hadn't called the island home from the age of sixteen until a few months after his *padré's* diagnosis, he couldn't ignore what had ultimately become a dying request. Not when the old man finally needed him.

"Stop that." Pepper laughed and snatched his hand. "You're being too quiet again."

"Sorry." He chuckled and picked up his pace, her eagerness to show him dolphins a potent draw. As he walked, elation filled him. He mentally rubbed his hands together, relishing the task ahead. He now had no problem with his arranged marriage, especially to one as beautiful and spirited as Pepper had already shown herself to be. Oh, yes, Ñico thought confidently. His plans were going exactly as planned.

Chapter 3

"That was fun. Where to now?" Pepper asked as she buckled her seat belt.

"How about a visit to Carne Point?" Nick nodded to the folded-up map the car rental company had provided. "It says in there visitors can hike through a wondrously preserved tropical hardwood grove. We can even tour the home of an early twentieth-century settler family."

"I'm game. I've never been."

"Great. It will be an adventure we can share together."

Minutes later, he parked, then reached into the backseat for his briefcase to retrieve a camera.

Both jumped out of the car together.

"Come on." He grabbed her hand once he made it to her side. "This should be educational."

Pepper laughed, enjoying his kid-in-a-toy-store-with-money-in-his-pocket enthusiasm. There was nothing sexual in his actions, which made him all the more attractive. Nick had been the perfect gentleman while touring the dolphin facility, his boyish curiosity sneaking out and lassoing her interest. This new side of him threw her off balance and changed their game, somehow. Pepper had never had so much fun, which made it hard to focus on her original purpose.

Nick brought a new dimension to how she viewed the Keys, one that continued when they walked through lush botanical gardens full of color—red hibiscus, pink fuchsias, orange and yellow lantana, blue clematis, green ferns—plants that grew in abundance in tropical locales and that she'd always taken for granted.

The afternoon had a magical air, like it was happening to someone else. Now, idly finishing the tour of the dark hardwood forests of mangroves and cypress, where damp muskiness had filled her nostrils, Pepper felt like she'd stepped into a fairy tale.

"You seem so interested in the wildlife," she said, noting his focused attention and long minutes spent reading information in front of the displays, just as he had at the Dolphin Research Center.

"I have a great appreciation for nature. I'm in the business of building and developing natural resources on beautiful pieces of property. Since man can't outdo nature, can in fact destroy it, I like seeing how others blend the two."

"Oh?" This was his first mention of anything personal. She knew next to nothing about Nick except that she found him sexually tantalizing as well as intellectually challenging. After all, he loved old movies. And she loved being with him. In hopes of learning more, she asked, "Do you work in Miami?"

"Sometimes." He nodded. "My company has an office in Hialeah." When she meant to ask him another question about his work, he nodded toward the water. "Stand over there, I want to get a picture." He clicked off a few shots as she mugged facetiously for the camera, then turned to a couple behind them. "Would you?"

Up until that moment, they'd kept their distance from each other. Yet, when Pepper felt his palm on the small of her back and he leaned in next to her, smiling, she sobered and all but forgot to breathe. What was it about this man who generated these feelings so effortlessly, she wondered, watching the lady who'd taken their picture hand the camera back to Nick.

Keeping one arm around her, he pocketed the camera, making no attempt to step away. Instead he turned to face her, placing his hand on her face, brushing stray, windblown hair behind her ear. His fingers then grazed her cheek. She observed his intent expression and forced herself to inhale air.

"Have dinner with me, *querida*."

It was not a question. His fiery gaze did things to her insides, causing her to look away. Geez, what a chicken she was, but sudden panic filled her. Nick was definitely better at playing the game, one that had taken a completely different turn somewhere during the day, and one she wasn't sure she could win any longer. She needed more time.

About to shake her head, a denial on the tip of her tongue, he stilled the movement with his thumb and forefinger, lifting her chin so that their stares reconnected.

"Before you speak, you should comprehend one thing."

While he held her gaze steady, she mutely peered into compelling ebony eyes. Eventually, she found her voice and was able to get out a weak, "What?"

"I won't take no for an answer."

Pepper bit her bottom lip, working to stop the smile from forming. What a stubborn Latino male he was, with such macho pride oozing from his expression. So like her father, leaving her no doubt as to the reason he attracted her in the first place.

Well, she was a stubborn Latina female and just the person to go head-to-head with him. She might be her mother's daughter but she wouldn't surrender the game so easily. Her resolve hardened. She'd have dinner with him, but a meal in a restaurant would be the only item on the agenda. Nick would just have to wait until she was ready for dessert.

His hand cupped her neck, while his thumb traced her top lip. His other hand stroked her back, as if to soothe her reluctance. Warmth spread from the contact, seeping into every cell of her body. So this was how the heroine on her in one of her old movies felt when being seduced. What a decadent feeling! Of their own volition, her lips parted in silent invitation. She watched as he lowered his head, moving in slow motion.

He groaned, just before his lips crushed hers.

Their earlier kiss had given her a taste of passion. With this kiss, it seemed as if passion exploded off the charts. Some of her resolve evaporated. Their few hours together had lowered her natural reserve and left this consuming need in its place. Pepper slid her hands around his neck and pulled him closer, unable to recognize the woman she'd suddenly become, one who couldn't seem to get enough of that mouth.

When she noticed the bulge between them, the heat of it scorched her, washing more warmth over her. He hadn't lied. He was huge. A moan floated past her ears. She was stunned to realize the sound had sprung from her lungs.

Nick broke the kiss, putting his forehead to hers. "Do you

feel why I can't take no for an answer?"

Nodding, she closed her eyes. She'd never felt this alive. Why did someone so similar to the men she'd gone to great lengths to avoid draw it out?

"Do you also understand, whatever is between us is growing?" he whispered. "This need is bigger than both of us." He leaned back. She knew he was studying her face. "Do you understand what I'm saying?"

Pepper kept her eyes shut tight, wishing for more time, but quickly realizing it was running out.

"*Querida*? Look at me."

The sultry quality in Nick's voice compelled her to obey. She opened her eyes, staring into a dark, penetrating gaze, an abyss stealing even more of her air.

"I want you. Can you feel how much?"

Mercy! Of course, she felt how much. She wanted him every bit as much, but she wasn't quite sure how to broach the subject of her lack of experience. She groaned inwardly. What a dilemma. "I'll have dinner with you on one condition." Old-fashioned or not, she wouldn't sleep with someone she'd known less than twenty-four hours. She wasn't a total idiot.

"Condition?" The sexy grin on Nick's face didn't ease her plight of getting her point across. "Why do I get the idea I won't like your *condition*."

The Spanish inflection he added to his last word sent tingles straight to her tummy. Forty-eight hours might even be pushing what she was comfortable with, but she didn't think either one of them would hold out for more than that, given all the electricity sizzling between them.

Pepper flashed her own smile at the thought, then sobered. "Yes, condition." A flush of heat rose up her face as she added, "I want one more day like today before we…you know…" She cleared her throat. "Do it." Another day like this one with him would go far, she realized, in enabling her to totally accept the idea of intimacy and also give her time to reveal her secret.

Nick cocked his head slightly and squinted, searching her face, scrutinizing every inch. The entire time, she held her breath.

Then his face relaxed and he nodded. "Okay. I accept your

condition, but I have one of my own."

Her lungs finally deflated in one huge sigh of relief. Remaining mute, Pepper raised her eyebrows, waiting for him to expand on his words. "Well?" she finally asked, raising her chin a notch when he still stared at her. "I'm listening."

"I don't believe this." He chuckled and shook his head.

Her eyes narrowed. "What's so funny?"

"You!" Nick snorted. "And me, allowing you to negotiate my seduction."

"Is that how you view me?" Pepper's back straightened. She felt her nails digging into her palms. "As a seduction?"

The question clearly brought him up short. He pondered it carefully, before his head moved slowly from side to side. "No. If only it could be so simple."

Silently, she concurred with his murmured confession. When he didn't say more, she prodded. "You had a condition?" She arched an eyebrow and bravely met his gaze.

"The entire evening is mine and you'll follow my lead."

His seductive smile set her on edge, causing wariness. She didn't trust it. She didn't trust herself. "I meant what I said." Her chin went up another inch.

Nick nodded. "I understand. I promise when we make love, you will want it as much as I do." He stepped away and held out his hand. "Come on. It's still early. Let's get a drink at one of those places on the water and get to know each other. After a long chat, we can watch the sunset from Sunset Park. Then we can have a late dinner. I have the perfect restaurant in mind."

"Okay." Pepper gripped his fingers, noticing once again the strength in them. The hand engulfing hers was warm, almost hot, his touch electric. Walking, she stared at her feet, fighting the sensations his nearness created. Being so close was like standing under an erupting volcano without bursting into flames because of the heat. How she managed to walk without revealing her thoughts, she had no idea.

~

"So, tell me something about Nick Guerrero."

Nico flashed his most self-deprecating smile. "I'm not that interesting."

"Oh, no." Pepper shook her head, grinning. She took a sip of wine, eyeing him. "Sell me something else. I'll never buy such a lame answer from someone like you."

He sighed, staring into the burgundy liquid, thinking. What could he reveal of himself? For some reason, he wanted to talk. Really talk. So that she would do the same. He'd never cared about what others he'd taken to bed thought. But he did now. He found his curiosity insatiable, especially as to why she left Isla del Diablo in the first place. He was so sure he'd made a similar impression during that last summer and she'd at least remember him, especially since she'd extracted his promise to wait until she grew up before he married. Of course that was the memory of a fifteen-year-old boy. He could understand if she'd changed her mind. After all, much can change in twelve years. But she hadn't even given him the courtesy of a meeting before she'd disappeared. Why had she run?

Pushing the disturbing thoughts away, he asked, "What would you like to know?"

"The usual stuff. Family, where you went to school, your work. I already know about a few of your extracurricular activities." His eyebrows rose, and she giggled. "Outside of sex."

Ñico chuckled. "My parents are divorced." Why had he mentioned that? His revelation concerned him, an idea reinforced when she reached across the table and squeezed his hand.

"I'm so sorry."

He mentally rolled his eyes, not wanting her pity. "It's not a big deal. It was a long time ago." He met Pepper's gaze and the sincerity he glimpsed in her warm brown eyes had him saying honestly, "No. That's not true. Their divorce did affect me." He brought his glass to his lips for a lengthy drink, using the task to contemplate. "I was sixteen. In one hour's time, my life changed. My family, consisting of two parents, one brother, and two sisters, was torn asunder. My sisters and I went to live with my mother. My father chose my brother." He swirled his wine, remembering. "I didn't realize until too late what that meant."

"What did it mean?"

Her soft question hung in the air, drawing another honest response. "As the second son, I became invisible." Ñico shrugged and smiled. "I can even admit, I was a bit defiant and wild."

His grin broadened at his understatement. Wild didn't begin to describe the hurt he'd tried to dull with alcohol and women. Over time, he'd only realized the lifestyle wasn't what he wanted, mainly because it never truly eased the pain. The women were all the same. Nameless, faceless entities, who never gave him what he searched for, and he grew tired of waking up with a pounding head and empty excuses on his lips. "I spent a long time acting badly in hopes of gaining his favor."

Ñico sighed. What a worthless waste of energy. He then had directed his anger toward making money instead, hoping that might work. Yet, other than making him wealthy, he might as well have not even bothered. Nothing had worked in bringing Ñico into his *padré's* focus until Juan died. And even then, he'd discovered he was only a fill-in for a dead brother. Juan had been the chosen one. Ñico was simply a substitute.

"Ah, something I understand."

He smiled. "Oh?"

"Yes. We share a commonality."

He quirked an eyebrow and spent a moment eyeing her. "I can't imagine you acting so stupidly." He chuckled and took another sip. "And I can't imagine anyone ignoring you."

Pepper's smile could only be called serene. "There are other ways of disappointing fathers. Sometimes one has to do what is best for her and go with her heart."

"And did you go with your heart?"

Shaking her head, she offered a stifled laugh. "No. My young heart was wrong, so I went with my mind instead."

Ñico's forehead furrowed, while his gaze narrowed. Her statement baffled him. Had she fallen in love with another? Is that why she defied her father and left the island? If so, she was unencumbered now. Is that why her heart had been wrong?

With her hand on her wineglass, fingering the stem, she studied him. "I see I've confused you." Her focus shifted to her wine. Pepper lifted the glass for a quick drink, then sighed. "But it's in the past and we were discussing you." Her smile reappeared, enchanting him. "Did you ever gain his favor?"

It was Ñico's turn to grin. "Let's just say I'm working on it."

She nodded. "Working on it? I see. And I gather your brother still has his favor?"

"No." His smile died. "Juan was killed in a boating accident." Which had left him as the only male heir. Yet, taking over the company wasn't enough. His father wanted a Fernández male grandchild to guarantee the empire he'd created, to continue his legacy for another generation. Ñico had argued his offspring might not be male and his sisters' boys were family, but Papa had been adamant. Having his heirs carry the Delgado blood of his best friend was only icing on an old man's cake, making Nico an even bigger hero in his *padré's* eyes if he honored his wishes. He'd probably attain sainthood if he and Pepper produced a male child within the year.

"I'm so sorry."

Her hand was back on his arm, squeezing. Remaining mute, he let the sound of her voice permeate his body and warm his heart. He heard sympathy in her words. And he could see it in her eyes, feel it in the soft squeeze of her fingers. Somehow, he sensed she also understood his feelings of family. He'd idolized his older brother, another reason he'd hated living in exile. But Juan had convinced him. The women in the family needed Ñico's male presence. Without his older brother or father, he'd accepted the role of protector.

"What about your mother? Your sisters?"

His smile returned full force. "I have their favor. Perhaps too much." Now his sisters had husbands who'd taken over his job and his mother had remarried. Yet all three had never ceased interfering in his life, always urging Ñico to find a good woman, settle down, and have *bambinos*. "How about you? Are you close to your family?"

Pepper's shoulders lifted in a subtle shrug. "I haven't seen them in a while. I communicate with e-mails and letters." She looked up, producing a sad smile. "Do you mind if we talk about something else?"

"I didn't mean to make you uncomfortable with my nosiness."

The waitress interrupted the moment, setting the bill next to him. "Just in time." He caught the woman's attention, then pulled out a credit card without looking at the folder, and handed both to her.

As the woman left, Ñico glanced at Pepper with eyebrows cocked. "Are you ready for the next phase of our evening?" When she nodded, a thought struck. His father was right. She *was* the perfect woman to bear his heirs. She'd be a good role model for their children. A picture of her pregnant with his babe entered his mind. He found the idea appealing. Very appealing. Too bad he didn't expect the appeal to last. A sobering thought for sure, but he had to face reality. By doing his duty, he'd have a family, but he'd lose interest.

As a man with a passionate appetite, no doubt he'd follow tradition and would eventually stray. In his world, men rarely remained faithful, something his father pointed out when he'd asked why he had to live in London with his mother after their divorce.

"And to keep things comfortable, we'll stay on less personal, safe topics," he said, shaking the disturbing thoughts. Right now, he'd focus on something more pleasant, like the moment he'd possess the beauty in front of him.

In minutes, he was leading her out the door.

~

"All the wine and champagne are making me light-headed." A small giggle caught her off guard. "I'm not used to drinking." Nick had already won the game, but with tonight's points Pepper felt as if she were the real winner.

She stifled another laugh and took a sip, using the movement to surreptitiously view the hunk lounging next to her. Nick had to be the most thoughtful man she'd ever met. Though, her list of those who'd offered it in her past was nil, she recognized a romantic when she spotted one. He'd gone to great lengths and paid special attention to details:

A beautiful sunset? Check.

A blanket on an ideal spot? Check.

Champagne and strawberries? Check and crosscheck.

Pepper looked out over the Gulf of Mexico, watching the vivid display Mother Nature provided.

"This is perfect."

She nodded and had to agree. It was a perfect evening to be out. The sky was still a crystal clear blue, not yet darkened by sunset. A few white clouds floated past, pushed along by strong air currents.

"Did you special order the sunset?"

"I see you've caught on to my strategy." Nick set his champagne aside. "But I can't take all the credit. Luck was with me," he whispered, planting a kiss on her cheek. His mouth lowered to kiss its way to her neck.

Delicate sensations swirled inside her belly. Her heartbeat quickened. Blood pulsed throughout and added to the flush of pleasure.

She grinned, only too happy to be alive. He was sexy and fun.

A spectacular performance of nature, a common sight most evenings, spilled from the west. Fading sunshine mixed with clouds, every so often interspersing bursts of light from heat flashes. She wondered why she'd never experienced such beauty with a man before now. As the sun lowered and slowly disappeared, Pepper couldn't stop one thought from forming. She felt a bond with Nick. As stupid as it sounded, she sensed a deep connection.

His lips finally settled over hers. At that exact moment, she fully comprehended how such blissful surroundings added to the surreal feeling, intensifying this invisible link.

~

The two stood on Pepper's porch later after a moonlit dinner, in yet another picturesque setting on a deck with the ocean as a backdrop. She glanced up at him, feeling slightly self-conscious all of a sudden. Thankfully, the light she'd left burning was only bright enough to barely illuminate the darkness, keeping them encased in shadows, so he couldn't read the discomfiture she knew was on her face.

The evening had been magical, just like the afternoon. Nick had done much to dispel her concerns. Despite her infatuation, she couldn't forget she'd known him for little more than twenty-four hours. Such a short time, but she felt as if she'd known him all her life. It seemed so stupid... cliché even, yet she felt as if he was the reason no other man had interested her. She'd been waiting for him, or someone like him. Was this how her mother had felt? Was Nick like her father? Was she destined to follow Elena Delgado's footsteps and have her heart broken?

Growing up, Pepper had continually heard the accounting of how Elena had fallen head over heels in love with Miguel Delgado at first glance. For years, her parents had seemed happy. Too bad Elena's days were now sorrow-filled, due to a philandering husband. Though her weekly letters always sounded upbeat, Pepper would never forget the day her mother had urged her to leave the island to escape the same outcome with an arranged marriage to a man who didn't deserve her. "Follow your heart," Elena had said at the airport, handing her the means to disappear and be independent almost four years ago. "Marry for love and marry a man who can be faithful. Only then will you be able to come home."

"You seem nervous."

Nick's voice pulled her out of her musings. His hands languidly stroked her arms and she trembled, lowering her eyes, not because of nerves, but because his nearness unsettled her.

He lifted her chin with a thumb and forefinger, causing her to meet his gaze. "You can trust me to keep my word, *querida*," he murmured, just before his lips found hers.

As earlier, his mouth consumed her, igniting the fire inside her belly. His tongue invaded, sending a burst of heat directly to her center, filling her with a desire she'd never before experienced, while also filling her with trepidation. He had it all wrong. She fully trusted him to keep his word. At this point, she was more worried about her own craving. She no longer trusted herself to keep to her original plan of remaining detached.

Pepper wasn't a fool. How could she feel secure in the ability to keep her feelings in check when there was so much about him that she couldn't resist? A new fear erupted along with the lava of want flowing through her veins. How would she ever survive once she'd given herself to him?

She needed to get away. To think. To ensure she wasn't making a huge mistake.

She broke the kiss, glancing down.

"No." The heated denial came out in a forced growl. "I won't let you deny what's there. Look at me, *querida*. See my need. See my wants." Nick's hand was under her chin again, lifting her head so she had no choice but to look into his ebony eyes, hot with desire. Then with his other hand he grabbed hers, placing it over his huge erection. "See what you do to me?"

Unable to keep the connection with his eyes, she closed hers, feeling more heat rise up her face. Pepper knew she shouldn't be aroused, but the move stirred her. She was dying to have him inside her, but she didn't dare. Not just yet. She prayed he would let her get away without spying the truth. His voice penetrated her thoughts, quashing her hopes.

"Look at me." He silently waited until she opened her eyes. The back of his hand slid gently up the side of her cheek as he held her gaze captive. "You can't hide what's in your eyes. Make up your mind, *querida*."

Nick kissed her again, spending a long moment making love with her mouth, eliciting her soft whimpers. Mercy, the man could kiss.

He lifted his head to break their connection and held his mouth a mere inch from hers. Seconds later, his tongue traced her lips and her low moan escaped.

When he used his tongue like that, she'd darn well promise him anything.

"I've met your condition and am giving you time." His lips grazed hers for the briefest kiss, drawing another moan. "I don't know if I can hold on to my patience for more than another day. What's more, I truly don't believe you want me to." His mouth then went back to tormenting her with its softness. This time when he broke away, he reached around her to open her door.

Nick nodded, giving her a searching look, before kissing her forehead. Then he placed his hands gently on her shoulders, turned her, and gave her a little push inside. "I'll be by at eight to pick you up for our day on the water."

"But I need to prepare," Pepper said, using the pretext to gain more time. "Fill up my tanks and—"

"I'll take care of everything. Just be ready." Nick cut off her words when she was about to add another excuse. "Sleep tight, *querida*. Enjoy your evening alone, because tomorrow night you'll have my company."

The next moment he was gone. She dreamily closed the door and leaned against the cool wood, smiling as memories of her day with him rolled over her. The man was intoxicating…maybe even habit-forming. Tonight she was more than tempted to open the door and drag him back inside.

Don't forget. Nick Guerrero is not long term.

Maybe not, she argued mentally. At least he'd make her first time memorable. That alone was worth a little heartache.

She heaved a contented sigh and started for her bedroom. Without the man's overwhelming presence, her mind cleared somewhat and rational thought returned. This feeling was only sexual awareness. He had the moves to make her heart race. Knew how to keep her hunger alive. Wasn't that exactly what she needed for her first time? And wasn't that why, despite relaxing, her body still felt slightly on edge?

She laughed and hugged herself. She could handle sex with Nick.

Pepper readied for bed. The warm sensations that had overwhelmed her earlier had subsided somewhat. Still, sleep eluded her. She couldn't quite quell the total excitement from her experience, and in those few moments of solitude, her need increased a hundred times. Her body suddenly tingled with awareness and desire. *Oh yeah!* She punched a pillow and tossed back and forth, working to get comfortable. She would handle sex with Nick because he'd become an unfulfilled addiction. At that moment, she could completely comprehend a junkie's need for a fix.

Chapter 4

"Right on time," Pepper said with a laugh after opening the door to Nick's hunky form the next morning. Then spying the coffee he carried, she put her hands together in prayer. "Thank you, Lord, for sending me a man who understands something so basic about me."

"A definite plus." Nick grinned, holding out his gift. "A man is not worthy of being called a man unless he understands the woman he means to make his."

"I do function better with a little caffeine," she murmured, grabbing the cup and ignoring the boastful statement, as well as the heat in his eyes. She had no plans to belong to anyone, but he didn't need to know that. "I didn't have time to make a pot and now we don't have to stop on the way."

"So do I get a good morning kiss as a reward?"

Pepper laughed and tamped down a surge of pleasure, unwilling to let his smile and flirting charm her. "Didn't you get enough kissing last night?"

"No. I'd never tire of kissing you."

Geez, the man had a smooth tongue. *He's probably said that to more women than the phone book holds.* Still, she couldn't quite suppress the little thrill the thought of him never getting enough of kissing her evoked, as Nick leaned in and playfully nipped at her lips. In seconds, he'd set both coffees aside, and his warm hands seized the sides of her face. Fingers plunged into her hair, undoing the scrunchie, allowing long masses of hair to fall free around her shoulders. His mouth covered hers, proving his declaration.

She certainly didn't think she'd ever tire of kissing him, especially when he drew her into his warmth. Sensation swamped her as more heat radiated between them. Nick released her face. One hand stroked her neck, while the other went to her breast. Bursts of pleasure shot everywhere, pulsating from the inside out.

He lifted his head, leaving her feeling bereft. But not for long. His mouth found her chin, continued caressing and kissing and nipping. First her neck, then all the way to her ear, where he spent a long moment adding his teeth and tongue, circling, biting, plunging. "See what you do to me?" He moved with the question, seducing her further. "I could kiss you all day. Every little bit of you."

A soft moan was her only answer. Pepper lost herself in his sensuous mouth, and couldn't help but wonder how it would feel for that mouth to replace his wandering hands. She couldn't muster enough energy to do much else than feel what his actions were doing to her insides.

Abruptly, he broke away and took a step back.

Disappointment overwhelmed her. Why was he stopping?

Nick ran his hands soothingly up her arms and gripped her shoulders. When he kissed her forehead, she opened her eyes, knowing frustration showed in them.

He cleared his throat, offered a lop-sided grin, and shrugged. "I know exactly how you feel, *querida*, but I did promise." He straightened, then held out her scrunchie. "Are you ready for another day in paradise?"

"All set." Pepper worked to keep her voice modulated. If he could act normal, so could she. She snatched the hair band and bent over at the waist to secure her hair, using the task to gain control of her senses. "I even have my swimsuit on underneath my shorts and t-shirt." Despite a pounding heart rate that might never return to normal, she grabbed her diving gear and pretended that gorgeous hunks showered her with compliments and kisses all the time. "Did you special order the day? Looks like a great morning for diving."

He nodded, relieving her of the heavy bag and securing it over his shoulder. "There's a stiff breeze, but the seas are flat." The usual calm seas of the shallow waters around the Keys meant clear water for their underwater experience.

"Yep," she said, going for more normal. "Makes for some awesome sailing." Talking about sailing and diving helped, even though her nerves were stretched so tight she felt as if she were ready to snap like a dry twig after a long drought. "Have you ever dived in the Keys?"

"No." Nick picked up her coffee and held it out.

"Be prepared for a treat." She latched on to the cup, thankful to have something to do with her hands.

"Ah, another adventure?" He nailed her with a hot gaze. "I look forward to discovering many new adventures with my lady today," he murmured, leaving her no illusion as to what he meant.

Nick seized her hand and held it firmly, while his thumb rubbed in a circular pattern in her palm before he lifted her wrist to his mouth.

Instantly, Pepper's mind went blank. Her lungs stopped working as air got stuck in the back of her throat. The entire time he kissed her wrist in that most sensitive spot, he kept his focus on her, as if saying this—everything up to now—was only a prelude to what his mouth and tongue would be doing—later.

"Are you ready?" Nick flashed a secret smile confirming her theory, before he turned, tugging the hand he still held.

Boy, was she ready! She had no other option but to follow him out the door.

As her wits slowly returned, Pepper wondered if she'd ever be normal again. She brushed a stray hair out of her face and gave up the pretense of not wanting to be his lady. She'd bask in the job as long as he allowed it.

~

The brisk breeze blew from the southwest, making their sail straight for Sombrero Reef a relatively easy one once they made it out of the channel.

"You didn't lie. You know your way around a sailboat." Pepper lounged against the deck cushion across from him.

Ñico smiled, not missing the bit of admiration in her voice. "I've sailed most of my life." He rather liked knowing she viewed his skill as admirable. He'd already found much to admire about her. "My brother taught me." His smile turned wistful.

The admission conjured up a picture of his older brother, who'd taken him out when he'd been six. Sailing and diving the waters around Isla del Diablo had been something they'd shared until Ñico's departure from his island home at sixteen. He'd kept his skills sharp at both during his long exile, with trips to other exotic places.

"Listen. Can you hear it?" he asked, pushing away the painful thoughts of his past. His grin returned, when she nodded enthusiastically. "There's nothing quite like the quiet surrounding the boat once you heft the sails and turn off the motor. I love the feel of them catching the wind, letting a bit of cloth power such momentum. I love everything about it."

"I know the feeling." Pepper's laugh floated on the breeze.

She shaded her gaze, which allowed him to peer into its brown depths. She had such lovely eyes. Expressive eyes. Eyes that said so much, now shouting amusement as well as contentment. A man could lose himself in those eyes.

"How about you?" Ñico's nod indicated the sails she'd effortlessly raised. "I can see you're quite a seasoned sailor yourself."

"I also have a brother who taught me."

"Brother?" This was the first time she'd mentioned anything personal about her family. "I see we share similar memories of siblings."

Suddenly a shadow of sadness crept into her features, making him wonder what put it there. Had something happened with her brother? Is that why she left Isla del Diablo?

"Oh, look." Pepper pointed to the water. "Dolphins." She rushed toward the bow and steadied herself with the stays, elegantly moving in tandem with the rise and fall of the boat as it cut through the swells.

Ñico remained at the helm, enjoying the view of her leaning over, her infectious excitement more potent than any aphrodisiac.

Two sleek dolphins breached the surface and blew double puffs, one right after the other. Their graceful leaps into the air appeared timed, as if dancing a duet as they swam with the boat.

"I'm impressed. How did you know to order them?" Pepper turned back to him with obvious pleasure in her eyes. "First a magical night and now this."

"You've discovered my secret." Ñico chuckled. "Stick with me, *querida*. I'm particularly gifted at ordering perfect sunsets, along with perfect sails."

"The perfect man." The smile she gave him made him feel

ten feet tall. "What will you do for an encore?" Then, as if realizing how suggestive her question was, she giggled. "Don't answer that. I already have a good idea."

Even from this distance, he could see a slight flush steal up her cheeks. Another chuckle erupted before he could stop it. *Dios*, if she didn't amuse him, draw out his laughter, and made him feel giddy. Made him feel like laughing more. Hell, she made him feel like dancing. His lady had the unique capacity to make him feel like braying at the moon.

Ñico stiffened. The realization had him sucking in a deep breath of air. Such feelings were new and unwanted. Why her? Why now? No woman had ever affected him like this. His eyes narrowed as he fought to understand what was happening to him. For a long while, he watched her exuberance in trying to reach for the dolphins as they swam alongside, breaching inches from the boat.

The image of that young girl returned, distorting the present and pulling him into the past. He found himself held under her spell.

Ñico blinked, shaking the strange thoughts.

That was it. The past intruded. Aided by the scenery. The sailing. The dolphins. Something about the tropical setting, along with his earlier memories, played with his senses. He needn't be concerned. Though an exceptional one, she was only a woman. A woman he meant to possess, but a woman nonetheless. Once he possessed her, his view of her would change. He was a male Fernández with full understanding of what that meant. His brother followed in his *padre's* footsteps; Ñico had no reason to doubt he'd act any differently. In all of his thirty-one years, no one woman had ever held his interest more than a few months. He certainly didn't expect miracles.

"*Sí, mi ángel pequeña*, Pepper," he whispered, watching her frolic with the sea creatures. Though she was no longer little, she was still his Angelina, and he'd have her. He'd possess her for however long it lasted. She'd give him an heir, maybe two, if he were lucky. But this feeling wouldn't last. His *padré* had taught him that. He pushed the thought away, suddenly not wanting to think about his desolate future.

"What a show." Pepper's animated laugh drew his gaze. Standing at the bow, she still had the look of the sea nymph she'd reminded him of as a young girl. "I love dolphins. It makes me think there is something out there—greater than us." Her hand made a sweeping motion, indicating the vastness of the blue seas to the east.

Ñico nodded and remained silent, observing as she made her way toward him using the rail to keep upright when the boat lurched.

"You're brooding again." Pepper plopped into the seat across from him. She shaded her eyes with her hand and studied him.

"Why do you say that, *querida*?"

"Because you haven't spoken a word in twenty minutes."

Ñico shrugged. "What if I have nothing to say?"

"No." She shook her head, her smile reinforcing her denial. "I don't believe you." Her intense gaze was back. "What are you thinking?"

He tightened his grip on the rail and wondered what she'd do if he told her the truth. And what truth should he tell her? That he was taken with her, his need to have her filling his soul. Or that he'd come to fulfill their bargain, the same one that he'd sealed with his father. His smile formed. "Okay. I admit. I was brooding."

Her quick laugh burst forth. "I knew it."

Pepper stretched long, tanned legs in front of her and pulled the t-shirt out of her shorts, lifting it over her head. The suit underneath was a modest one-piece. Yet nothing could hide the generous curves of her breasts, which were emphasized more when the scrap of fabric holding her hair came loose and lustrous, waist-length tresses fell around her shoulders.

Dark wisps cascaded everywhere, filling his senses with the need to see if they were as soft as they appeared, blanketing the round mounds with strands of vibrant texture. The sunlight reflecting off her hair accentuated the color's richness from cinnamon highlights on top to deep bronze in the middle to black, dark as night, underneath. Black didn't seem an adequate description for such a lovely shade.

It took all his willpower not to reach out and touch.

48

"But I have to tell you, you do brooding really well."

Ñico glanced up at the sound of her low voice, noting the teasing glint in her eyes. She leaned over him and planted a kiss on his nose. "So Latin and sexy as hell." She lounged back into the cushions, set the shirt aside, and grabbed the sunscreen. First she squirted lotion on her arms, rubbing the white cream into her skin with slow easy strokes. Then, after discarding her shorts, she slathered lotion on her thighs, stealing his breath as she repeated the slow strokes, working from the top of her legs to her feet. Such sexy feet, her red polished toenails prominently highlighted, as she arched each foot while rubbing. Finally she added a bit of lotion to her face, leaning her head back and closing her eyes as she spent long seconds blending it into her hairline and over her throat with more slow, sure strokes. Her fingers slipped inside the edges of her bodice as she rubbed lotion onto her chest

Clenching his hands to keep from grabbing her and showing her what her actions were doing to him, Ñico's focus remained on her. He bit back a laugh, steeling his efforts not to rise to her unbeknownst baiting until she held up the bottle, her expression saying, *Would you?*

"Sure. Just let me trim the sails and set the autopilot." He stifled another urge to touch her, as she set the lotion in the cup holder, inches from him. If he touched her now, he wouldn't be able to stop at touching. Taking a deep breath, working to gain control of his wits, he spent a moment checking the wind direction and watching the luffing mainsail until it filled completely with air and he adjusted his position. He flipped on the autopilot, punched in his coordinates, and reached for the sunscreen.

Ñico poured out a liberal amount in the palm of his hand as Pepper presented her back. She had a beautiful back. Feminine. Slender and willowy. An elegant feline entered his mind, as his fingers met with skin. He rubbed the lotion in, wondering if he could make her purr.

The sails luffed and snapped with the wind. The boat cut through the light chop, its minimal lurching and rocking adding to the seductive quality of the moment.

"Hmmm." She sighed, her expression so serene while he caressed her back for long seconds, letting his fingers roam. The stiff breeze blew her hair about. He brushed it aside, wanting to wrap those strands around his hand and pull her to him.

Water slapped at the sides of the boat and was the only sound. The scent of lotion mixed with Pepper's spicy perfume permeated his already heightened senses. His body was on fire with need.

"Thanks."

The one word spoken so succinctly filled the space around him and rolled over his senses.

He smiled. His goddess had no idea of her effect on him. Once done with his ministrations, he grazed the edge of her suit with a fingertip, fighting the desire to slip a hand beneath to stroke her warm skin. He gripped her shoulders, gently pushing ribbons of soft hair out of the way, and kissed her now exposed neck.

She eased out of his grasp and nodded. "Turn around. I'll return the favor."

Though slightly disappointed, Ñico yanked off his polo shirt. He rarely used sunscreen, given his dark complexion, but he wasn't fool enough to pass up such a prime opportunity. He'd use any excuse to have her hands on his body.

"You have the right touch, *querida*." He totally enjoyed her languid strokes.

"I love touching you."

He honed in on the suggestive tone. This was the first time since yesterday morning she'd taken the initiative, and he found himself responding, the effects hard to hide with just swim trunks on.

"You're so powerful. Strong."

The awe in Pepper's voice had the blood pounding in his ears, a freight train of desire hitting him head on. "See what you do to me, *querida*," he whispered. "I'm dying to be inside you."

She cleared her throat and turned away, as color rose in her cheeks.

He used the pads of his fingers to brush a blowing strand of hair behind her ear. Ñico let them slide the length of her cheekbone to her neck. Then he lifted her chin, forced her to look into his eyes. "But I gave you my word. You would want to make love as much as I." He waited a heartbeat and asked, praying for a yes. "Do you?"

Her tongue nervously slid over both lips, before she bit the bottom one, indecision clearly written over her features. "I'm…um…I…" Pepper glanced at her fingers, studying them intently without adding anything further. More color infused her cheeks.

He smiled. She seemed hesitant and magnificent, a heady and frustrating combination.

"So soft," he murmured, pulling her onto his lap, unable to stop from kissing that sexy mouth, despite her unease. Before he lost himself in the kiss, he broke away and hugged her fiercely. He rested his chin on her head and pushed need away.

Nico had promised to go slowly, and she was wavering. For some reason, he needed her to want him as much as he wanted her, without hesitation. Why it mattered, when it never had in the past, he didn't know. He only knew how he felt.

~

They sailed the remaining distance to Sombrero Reef and anchored to a mooring, making good time. Like Nick, Pepper presented a cool façade after their hot encounter, both pretending as if the heat had never erupted.

Thankful to finally have an ocean's distance between them, Pepper quickly donned her equipment, also thankful that they needed partial wet suits. Nick was hard enough to ignore wearing only swim trunks. Thirty-two feet might offer plenty of room to move about, but the sloop was just too confining. She'd acted like a complete ninny and wanted to disappear. The minute she revealed her secret, he'd really think her one. What she wouldn't give to have even one lover under her belt.

She'd already bungled her first attempt at trying to act seductive. Just remembering her awkward effort had heat streaking up her face. Yet, she hadn't lied when she'd blurted out her thoughts. He was strong. Like some graceful big cat—a jaguar or cougar came to mind—lean, but muscular and powerful. She had no illusions over who would be king of the jungle, if Nick roamed it.

She couldn't stop the rush of excitement over the thought of spending the day with him. They shared so many passions.

Sailing…diving…old movies…even dolphins. Who was this man with unending patience and so in tune with her? This paragon who made her heart skip beats?

Pepper had no more time to think on it because, suddenly, he stood right in front of her offering a helping hand as she slipped into her buoyancy vest, then readied her tank and regulator.

"The water's so clear." Nick situated his tank. "It reminds me of home."

"You live near a reef?"

"I did when I was younger, before my parents split up." He grinned. "England's channel isn't quite as inviting. Neither is the Thames."

"I've never been. Is that where your mother lived? England?"

"Yes. In London. I went to university at Oxford. If not for my dark skin and slight accent, I could pass for an Englishman."

"No." Pepper shook her head, holding on to her grin. He didn't look like any Englishman she'd ever met of those who'd passed through Second Chances. Now, a Spanish conquistador she could believe. "You could pass for a native Floridian."

Nick ignored her comment, turning his attention to the structure jetting out of the water, and pointed. "That's an interesting lighthouse."

"It was constructed in the eighteen sixties." Nodding, she shaded her eyes with a hand. "Be prepared for a treat. This reef is home to all kinds of corals—elkhorn, staghorn, brain, and every kind of tropical fish. Because it's so shallow, the light penetrates and offers a unique setting."

"I can't wait." He motioned at the tank on her back. "Is your air on?"

"Of course. I've gone through my checklist."

"Good. I know we'll be in around twenty feet of water, but we've never dived together. We should go through the hand signals, so we're in sync."

She nodded. They quickly went through each one.

"Remember, stay with me. I'm your buddy."

"Don't worry." She laughed. "I'm fully certified and I *do* know the rules."

The cool blue water felt invigorating. Pepper adjusted her

mask and cleared her ears, as they went lower in their wonderland of color. Yellows, corals, and reds came into focus as fish darted about, separated, then came back together once she and Nick were out of range.

He stopped and pointed. Through her mask, her gaze followed his fingers. An inquisitive barracuda swam toward a school of grouper. Both species were abundant in the vertical relief and sandy channels of the reef. As if a silent command had been issued, the grouper split into two schools, leaving a wide berth for the predator. At the same time, smaller fish, or parasitic feeders feasting off the larger fish, gave Pepper and Nick a fascinating demonstration of a symbiotic relationship in action.

Nick moved on and drifted near the coral, poking into various crevices and hiding spots, looking at neon gobies and juvenile Spanish hogfish lurking near the large brain and star coral's protection. Noting the awe in Nick's wide eyes peering through his mask, she viewed her favorite diving spot through a new perspective while showing him a reef she loved. The sun glinted with penetrating light due to the shallow depths; the only sound the *whoosh* from their regulators as they breathed slowly in and out while they explored.

Though a dozen or so other boats had also moored above them, they didn't see another soul while under, making her realize the true vastness of the underwater sanctuary.

Pepper finally broke the surface, lifted off her regulator, then her mask. Leaning her head back in the clear water, she used the moisture to untangle the straps from her long hair. Nick trailed behind. The water their ascent disturbed lapped against the sailboat, rocking it as she treaded water. They'd been under for almost sixty minutes, most of the time never venturing lower than ten or twelve feet.

"What a dive." Her short laugh followed the exclamation. They could have remained longer without worrying too much about nitrogen levels, but they'd gotten in a fantastic hour. "Awe inspiring."

"I couldn't agree more." He swam to the ladder, and holding on to a rung, maneuvered out of his vest with tank, setting it on the dive platform. Pepper unzipped her vest and shrugged it off and he reached over and assisted her with the heavy equipment, placing it with his own. Then, with the strength and grace of the cat she took him for, he eased out of the water, using his arms to haul himself onto the boat, while Pepper slipped off her swim fins.

After helping her onto the platform, Nick secured the dive gear. Pepper watched his efficient rinsing it of salt water, wondering how to broach the subject of her virginity. She hadn't missed the little signals he'd sent during the dive. Being underwater obscured them somewhat, much like a thin, distorting veil. Yet Pepper could only marvel at how their surroundings had increased the awareness of the other senses, especially when he'd touched her. The dive had been a prelude to his lovemaking. Oh, how she wanted to make love with him.

Her gaze narrowed, zeroing in on those hands. Strong hands. Sensitive hands. Hands she had no doubt would do much to make her first time memorable. Her gaze shifted, traveling higher to his face. She swallowed hard, unable to look away. Nick didn't break eye contact as he shut off the nozzle and walked purposefully toward her.

He stopped inches from her. His fingers pushed a lock of hair behind her ear, before sliding down and gripping her shoulders. As if they had a mind of their own, her lips parted, answering his silent request. Quickly his mouth descended over hers, nibbling gently, sucking softly, biting tenderly, giving her a generous taste of his passion.

Yells and jeers burst into her consciousness just then. She stiffened and stepped away. A boat bobbing nearby drew her attention, its deck filled with divers looking their way.

Nick lifted his head, turning in the direction of the boisterous voices. His smile appeared, and he quirked an eyebrow. "Friends of yours?"

"No." How embarrassing. "I have no idea who they are." This wasn't the time or the place to drop on the deck and have her way with him. Not in broad daylight with an audience of crazy tourists. Pepper cleared her throat and prayed the heat she felt going up her face wasn't noticeable.

"Then why do you care what they think?"

Long strands of her dark hair, now dry, flew in the stiff

breeze. He caught most, lightly wrapping the length around one hand. His other hand cupped the back of her neck and barely rubbed, offering a demonstration of the power his fingers wielded in adding pleasure with his soft touch. She stared at the horizon, wishing she could maintain control when he was near.

"Pepper?"

The whispered question drew her gaze. As much as she wanted to keep her unease of the situation hidden, so Nick wouldn't see how disconcerted she truly was, she couldn't stop the truth from showing in her eyes.

"I don't understand. You seem fearful. Are you afraid of me?"

"No. Of course not." She was much more fearful of her own mushrooming desire. This need for him swamped her. Made her feel entirely out of her element. Her head went from side to side as she squeezed her eyes shut to block him from glimpsing further into her soul.

Remember, Pepper. He's only a brief affair, not a soul mate.

If that was so, then why did she find the thought of a brief affair with him disturbing? And what would happen to her if, when he was gone, this yearning never ended?

He saw too much.

Pepper pulled out of his grasp and pivoted, running below as fast as her legs would carry her. She already felt unprepared for what he'd think when he finally realized the truth of her inexperience, not to mention this all-consuming craving.

Her back was to the steps leading into the galley and she heard nothing of Nick's approach, but Pepper sensed him behind her. She reached for her cover-up and threw it over her shoulders in a useless attempt to hide her quivering body.

"You can't run from your desires, *querida*." The low statement confirmed his presence, quashing her hopes that she could somehow escape total humiliation unscathed. "I have no intention of hurting you. I want to love you."

She closed her eyes, allowing the silky warmth of his voice to stroke her. A soft smile formed. Love. That's what she craved. Oh, how wonderful it would be if he could love her in the true sense of the word. She was a fool. No different from her mother. How stupid to even consider such a thing was possible after knowing someone for less than forty-eight hours.

His hands gripped her shoulders, slowly turning her. Nick lifted her chin with a thumb and forefinger, leaving her no choice but to meet his searching gaze.

"I believe you feel what I feel." Still eyeing her, he waited a heartbeat, then asked, "Do you?"

She nodded. "I feel it," she admitted. Why lie? He had to glimpse what was in her heart when he peered into her eyes.

"Is it so bad to use our bodies to express our feelings?"

"No." Pepper shook her head. Her smile spread. Mercy, did her body have a yearning to express itself. She heaved a long, drawn-out sigh. Might as well get it all out. "It's just that I've never expressed myself in quite that way before," she murmured, averting her gaze and twining her fingers together. She studied her fingernails, waiting for him to say something…anything. When Nick remained silent, she slanted a furtive glance in his direction. Yep. Her revelation had definitely thrown him off balance. "Don't look so shocked. It's not as if I have a disease or something."

"You're a virgin?" he asked slowly.

"Yes," she replied when the look on his face demanded substantiation. "I'm a virgin." There. She said it.

His hand shot through his hair, landing on the back of his neck. He rubbed, as if kneading would help him understand.

Geez! How hard was it to figure out? Nick would be her first. "If it's too much to handle, I'll understand."

"*El cielo me ayuda*," he whispered. He muttered another Spanish phrase, this one not so nice, and began to pace in the small space.

"I'm sure help from heaven isn't the answer to my problem, nor is swearing." Pepper watched him struggle a few more seconds, noting his pure discomfort. She grinned. "Sex is."

That comment got his attention. He stopped in midstride and his focus landed on her face. His eyes narrowed, adding to his skeptical expression.

"What? Now you don't believe me?" Pepper shrugged. "Such cynicism, Nick. It's not like I can hide it. You're going to find out soon enough."

"I…how…I…" He stopped and shook his head. "I don't know what to say."

"How about, 'It's okay.' Or, 'It doesn't change anything.'"

"Now, that's where you're wrong. It changes *everything*."

As always, the bit of inflection in the last word sent a surge of pleasure through her that hadn't completely ebbed when he walked the few steps separating them, holding her gaze captive. He stopped inches from her, his dark gaze burning hotter.

"I will be gentle on your first time, *querida*, and though I yearn to be inside you, a boat is not the place for such a momentous occasion. Also, I think it best that you thoroughly know me before you consider giving yourself to me."

If Nick's looks hadn't heated up her blood, his whispered, accented promise certainly did.

"You're sure?" She worked to keep the frustration out of her voice. At this very moment, she knew him well enough to know it would be an experience of a lifetime. Besides, now that she'd unveiled her secret, she had a hankering to get *it* over with, in order to see what she'd been missing.

"Oh yes, I'm sure." His lips then lowered. His fingers plowed through her hair. This time his mouth was exactly as he'd said…gentle…and so inviting. Pepper moaned, wrapped her hands around his neck, and pulled him closer. She could kiss him all day. A lifetime or longer. Just like this.

Nick lifted his head and smiled. "We should head back now." After a few more light kisses, he straightened.

She nodded. When he stepped away, dropping his arms to his side, disappointment, as well as the handful of hair he released, settled over her back like a shroud of finality.

She stood immobile as he turned and started up the stairs to the deck.

The sail back to shore was more torturous than anything Pepper had endured before. Anticipation of what lay ahead shone in Nick's every glance, in his every touch. By the time they motored into the harbor, Pepper felt as though she were a tightened bowstring, waiting.

She jumped off the boat, working to secure the lines, hoping the chore would create some distance. He clearly had a stronger will than she, considering she'd have caved hours earlier. As far as she was concerned, a boat seemed the perfect place for what she had in mind.

"Do you need help?" he asked, when she slowed with the last line, taking her time as images of what she'd do to him when she got the chance flitted through her mind.

She shaded her eyes from the sun and looked up, spying the gorgeous hunk, smiling at her in a way that said he knew her thoughts. Knew of her discomfort.

Pepper shook her head no, wondering how he remained so calm. She'd seen Nick's desire now and again during the return sail. It wasn't as if he'd been able to hide it. At those times, the sensual tension on the boat had grown thick. The air had crackled with a sexual expectancy, leaving a charged current of attraction or force field in its wake.

All he'd done in response was smile and kiss her in that mind-numbing way of his, wiping all thought from her brain. And then he'd lift his lips and turn his attention back to the knot meter, the autopilot, or one of the sails, pushing his need away the same way a stuffed eater pushed away an empty plate.

How he'd been able to do it and remain aloof, she had no idea.

Seconds later, he stood next to her, taking her hand. "Come on, *querida*. Let's go check in the boat and then I'll drop you by your place so you can dress for dinner."

"Drop me off at my place?" This so wasn't going her way. Maybe she could entice him.

"Don't look at me like that. We are not making love until I woo you properly."

Chapter 5

Pepper was still a virgin. Ñico could barely believe such a thing possible for a normal, sexy, twenty-five-year-old woman in this day and age. The knowledge still filled him with awe, especially after spending time with her.

"How did you know about this place?" The admiration in Pepper's voice stroked something deep inside of Ñico. That sensitive part he'd kept hidden from the world. He ignored the warning twinges that had accompanied his thoughts all too often in the last twenty-four hours, too caught up in how good it felt to see her smile. With anyone else he'd have walked away, rather than further open that side of himself.

This instance was different; the woman sitting across from him, with her eyes feasting on the idyllic sunset, was to be his wife. His acceptance of it all should worry him. That it didn't should worry him even more, but he shrugged off all concerns. He was simply having too much fun to pay any heed to his misgivings.

He planned to give her a proper courtship, become monogamous, and pretend it would always be so. If anything, she would have wonderful memories of their time together in paradise to last a lifetime. And so would he. Yet, five days into their courtship and he was more enamored of Pepper than of anyone he could remember in the last ten years.

"You could write a tourist's guide book on the Florida Keys."

"I told you I'm on a fact-finding mission." Ñico chuckled when her eyebrows rose. She definitely expected him to expand on his comment, always pressing him for details of his background. "I fully educated myself before I stepped off the plane a week ago. Running an island business means that I am always looking at ways of increasing tourism. I've seen the ill effects of too many other islands that have grown too fast."

"Just where is this island?"

"A short plane ride from Miami." The music started a samba. He stood and held out his hand, more to avoid the questions that were sure to come than a wish to get close to her. "Would you like to dance?" Holding her in his arms when he had to leash in the desire strumming through him was pure torture. He didn't know how long he could hold out without making Pepper his. He wanted her agreement to marriage before he consummated their relationship. Why it mattered, he didn't know. He just knew it was important.

Pepper's smile zinged his insides with more heat. Stilling all thoughts of lust, he placed his hand on the small of her back, led her to the dance floor, and finally wrapped her in his embrace. A whiff of her delicate perfume wafted under his nose when he grazed her forehead with a quick kiss. His grip on Pepper tightened. At the same time, he strengthened his resolve and guided her around the floor.

The slow love ballad eventually faded. Ñico released Pepper and steered her back to the table before she had a chance to ask for another dance. He couldn't hide his reaction to her and thought it best to steer away from bodily contact for the time being.

He held her chair out and waited for her to sit before easing into his own chair. "I'm curious, Pepper."

Her hand rested on the stem of the wineglass. She fingered the rim and looked up at him with that gorgeous dark gaze. His mind went numb.

"What are you curious about?" she asked when he remained silent for several long seconds.

Ñico cleared his throat. "Why, if you love animals so much, don't you own a cat or a dog?" The subject had to take his mind off of taking her to bed. It hadn't escaped his notice during their short time together that she made time for every dog and cat they came into contact with. She fed several stray cats around her restaurant and talked to them as if they were good friends. Her soft heart for them warmed his heart, made him think she'd be a loving mother. He shoved the thought away. Thinking about making a baby with her didn't help lower his libido one bit.

She shrugged. Her smile turned wistful. "I'd love to adopt a pet, but I'm allergic to cats, and since I work long hours with little time off, it wouldn't be fair to own a dog."

Ñico nodded. Somehow he made it through the rest of their meal, but it was getting harder and harder to ignore her allure. He had to put some distance between them—and fast.

He paid the bill and escorted her to his rental car that the valet had just driven up. Neither spoke on the drive to her house. He pulled in to her driveway and shut off the engine, the silence deafening, which only highlighted the sexual tension that hummed in the air.

At Pepper's porch, he opened her door and turned to leave.

"Is something wrong?"

He spun back around and glanced at her expression. Hurt gleamed in her eyes.

His shoulders slumped. "Nothing's wrong, *querida*."

"Then why the quick brush-off? You look like you're going to a fire and can't get away fast enough."

Ñico bit back a frustrating laugh. If she only knew. "I think it's time you know my intentions."

Her gaze narrowed and she studied his face. "Intentions?"

"I'm an honorable man."

When he didn't explain, she prodded, "And?"

"You've been saving yourself and I refuse to ruin you without some sort of commitment."

Pepper laughed. "That's so Latin, not to mention archaic." When he didn't smile, she sobered. "Oh my God, you're serious, aren't you?

"Very." Ñico nodded. "What can I say? I *am* Latin, and archaic or not, it's non-negotiable. If we make love, I want the promise of a future with you. I was hoping you'd want the same thing."

Her jaw dropped and her mouth opened into that perfect, understanding O as realization hit. She stepped closer and wrapped her arms around him. "You're sure?"

Her mouth grazed his. Teasing and enticing. He curled a fist and closed his eyes, fighting desire. It was as if she were testing his restraint and this meant too much to him to fail now. He felt confident she'd willingly agree to be his wife before they made love, but the wooing was killing him.

Pepper let go when he didn't respond. "What if I don't want to get married?"

"Then we don't make love. It's that simple." It may turn out to be an empty threat, but she didn't need to know that.

"Wow! I can't believe this." She rubbed her forehead with both forefingers before glancing his way again. "Why can't it just be an affair?"

Nico shrugged. "You should ask yourself why you waited so long." He hesitated. "Think about it tonight. I don't want to continue seeing you if I'm just an affair." He turned and, taking the biggest risk of his life, walked away.

~

Nick wanted marriage? An ultimatum straight from the script of one of her old movies.

Pepper stood watching the taillights from Nick's car disappear as his parting shot registered. She barely knew him, but deep down, she *knew* him. His personality drew her. She felt whole when she was with him. He reminded her of the men she'd grown up with. Real men, not afraid to show their feelings, and she had to admit, being with him fed something in her soul that had been missing since she'd left home. In the ensuing four years, she no longer took the time to play or do the things she used to enjoy.

Pepper never had a lot of friends because her parents' wealth separated her from the locals on the island where she grew up. In college, she discovered a lot of girls just like her and made a ton of friends.

She now had Rachel and Karen, who were closer than sisters. The three shared one thing in common, though. They were each running from a past and wanted to create their perfect future in the Keys. Though small, Grassy Key and Marathon were big enough to hide in plain sight, which is exactly what she'd been doing, Pepper suddenly realized. Maybe it was time to quit hiding.

She headed into the kitchen and grabbed the brownies she'd baked earlier. With plate in hand, she opened the patio door, strode outside, and sat at the table. A warm, humid breeze stirred the tree leaves and the insects were singing their nightly tunes. She took a bite and thoughtfully chewed as she stared off into the horizon, reflecting on Nick's proposal.

How she could even be considering it baffled her, but she couldn't dispute the fact that the idea had merit. The more Pepper was with Nick, the more she came to like him. The first week of her vacation was almost over and she hadn't been this relaxed in years.

They'd been together daily and she was already infatuated with him. Whether it was true love or not, she didn't know. All she knew was that she'd never felt so needy or so cherished. Nick had a way of making her feel as if she were the only interesting thing on the planet. She loved the attention and had forgotten how much she missed male companionship.

But you don't really know him. You don't know where he came from or all that much about him.

She had to be crazy to even consider the idea, but she couldn't dismiss the possibilities. He was one sexy male and she wanted him to be her first. So what if they got engaged. She would just make sure the wedding date was far enough into the future to give her time to discover if marriage to him was what she really wanted.

Pepper smiled and took a bite. That was a doable plan. They'd both get what they wanted out of the deal. She rubbed her arms and hugged herself, totally satisfied with her decision.

"Nick Guerrero, you are mine," she said before taking another bite of brownie.

Chapter 6

Ñico opened his hotel room door and waited for Pepper to go in ahead of him.

"This is nice." She walked through the suite, giving the rooms a thorough scan. In the bedroom, she advanced to the sliding glass doors that provided a panoramic view of the ocean. "I've never been in one of these suites before."

"It serves its purpose," Ñico replied, eyeing her thoughtfully. She appeared slightly nervous, smoothing nonexistent wrinkles off her shorts. He cared little for the view, other than having her stand in front of it, preferably naked.

He smiled, thinking of the evening ahead. They'd spent the day windsurfing and sunbathing, and now he had her all to himself. Even better, she'd agreed to his terms. Imagine. His wild angel agreed to marry him and he'd be her first. He considered it an honor, one he would treasure. Always.

Pepper cleared her throat. One hand moved to her lustrous hair, still smoothing. "So what's on the agenda for this evening?" The minute the question was out, she realized what she just said and a dark blush highlighted her cheeks.

His grin spread. He slowly strode toward her, letting his thoughts show in his eyes. "I'm sure you must have a clear idea, *querida.*" Finally, he had her all to himself in a room conducive to romance, including an inviting king-size bed, along with a gigantic whirlpool tub they'd make use of later. He'd already ordered dinner to be served by candlelight on the terrace, also for later, as he intended nothing to interrupt his plans right now.

"You have no need to fear, we're to be married soon." Ñico halted inches from her, continuing to hold her gaze. "My agenda includes satisfying all our appetites."

Awareness dawned on her face, drawing an urge to hug her. *Dios*, she was so adorable. He lowered his head. She watched with eyes wide open as their lips touched. He had no idea whether or not she'd closed them because the only thought streaking through his mind was having her naked underneath him. He'd spent too much time subduing his need that it took an intense effort to remain calm and collected.

His hand found the bit of elastic securing her glorious hair. Releasing the sleek mane, his fingers plummeted through silky tresses, yielding handfuls of softness, while their mouths and tongues converged. He loved her waist-length hair now intertwined in his hands and her generous mouth that melded with his. The sensuous sound of her low moans scraped at his yearning, leaving him open and raw with desire.

For tormenting days Ñico had stoked her passion, but in doing so, had stoked his own. He'd become a smoldering mass of need, a need ready to erupt into flames and one he couldn't fight any longer.

"Do you see what you do to me?" he whispered, settling between her legs, that perfect spot that her tall height made possible. He groaned, moving closer, at the same time kissing and nipping his way along her neck, continuing to her ear. "I'm so ready to make you mine."

Another moan was his only answer. He closed his eyes, still fighting a craving that caught him by surprise with its intensity. It took a few seconds before he dared allow his mouth to descend over hers again.

Ñico guided Pepper to the bed and focused on maintaining an unhurried impression, so as not to alarm her with this burgeoning drive to mate. The brush of her body stroked him with each step they took, inflamed him more, and made him doubt his ability to keep to his resolve of going slowly this first time.

At the bed's edge, he broke the kiss to divest her of her t-shirt and shorts. Aided with a little push, she fell back against the pillows, a burst of laughter upon her lips. He shrugged out of his own shirt and swimsuit, leaving him naked. She still wore the one-piece suit, all legs and arms and a bit of color. He sent up a silent prayer, thankful the scrap of material helped in his attempt to hold his need in check, preventing him from sinking into her warmth. For the time being.

Go slow and give her pleasure first.

Nico tried to focus on the mantra, but his control was shot. He couldn't stop from touching and kissing her, just as she was doing to him. Despite her lack of experience, Pepper was too intoxicating to ignore.

He broke the kiss. "No fair," he growled, fingering the suit's strap on her shoulder. His hand slipped under the yielding fabric. Then rolling, he positioned her underneath him. "I'm naked and you still have this on." Breathing heavily, he tugged the strap down her arm, releasing a lush, round breast in the process. He bent to take it into his mouth. Her low moan registered, inciting him further. His other hand pushed the remaining strap. Seconds later, she was as naked as he.

Go slow and give her pleasure first. Somehow he couldn't concentrate on his directive, especially when her hands and lips kept moving over him.

"Please. *Querida*," he whispered, breaking contact and gripping her hand, one that wouldn't stop tormenting him. "I'm close to losing control."

"Isn't that what makes great sex?" Pepper pulled her hand from his and trailed a finger along his ribcage. "Losing yourself in your lover?"

"Yes."

Nico sucked in a deep breath and blew it out as her hand roamed lower, fingers wrapping around his fullness. He chuckled and groaned at the same time, working to ignore the intense pleasure her hand was generating. In seconds, it was no longer a laughing matter. If she didn't stop, he would self-destruct.

"This is your first time," he ground out in an effort to warn her. "I want to make it memorable, not painful." His wild angel wasn't cooperating.

Pepper laughed. The sound shot straight through his ear, traveling in a path of liquid heat all the way to his groin. He held his breath to keep from exploding and embarrassing himself. *Dios*, this wasn't going the way he thought it should. "You have no idea how close to the edge I am." Nico lifted up on one forearm, stilling her stroking fingers with the other hand, while catching her heated amber gaze with his. "You're driving me wild. If I don't slow down, I may hurt you."

"Okay." She swallowed hard, worked to tug her hand free, and eyed him warily, as if suddenly grasping the seriousness of his warning. "I'll slow down."

Ñico grinned when she completely stilled her efforts.

"You are so beautiful." He let his gaze roam over her perfect body, now flush with sensual excitement. He intended to make it perfect for her. Only she obviously had other ideas as her hands and lips now assaulted him and stripped all thought from his mind when she reached for him and guided him home. Until he felt her flinch. He halted in midstroke, using every bit of restraint he could muster and rose onto his forearms.

He gritted his teeth and looked at her face. "Are you okay, *querida*?"

Pepper presented a generous smile and nodded.

She relaxed and he drew out, stopping at the edge. Then, slowly he pushed in, rocking at the same time, repeating the languid strokes until she was joining him, at which point his control snapped. Ñico's thrusts intensified, his body no longer responding to his mental orders to be gentle. To slow down. Not when she met him with her own unrestrained passion. When her release came, his orgasm hit with a force he'd never experienced until now.

As the last twinge of sensation died, he collapsed on top of her, unable to move.

For a long while, neither stirred. He rolled, bringing her on top, unwilling to lose the connection he felt with her.

"That was amazing." She laughed and lifted up.

Ñico chuckled and pulled Pepper closer to kiss the top of her head. "It was amazing." His smile became smug. "I'm just glad you finally said yes to my marriage proposal."

She rolled her eyes and gave a derisive snort. "You used underhanded means. Heck, I bet you're just macho enough to think you've won something, aren't you?"

"Damn right!" For some reason her description fit. He planted another kiss on her nose, grinning. "*Sí, mi pequeña ángel. I've won your hand in marriage and I'm you're first.*" *And last,* he wanted to add but didn't because she'd have every right to expect the same.

Her eyebrows rose a good inch.

"Admit it." Ñico lifted up to nuzzle her neck, chuckling harder. "You've given me something precious." Damn, if she didn't make him want to laugh, even after one of the best sexual experiences of his life and the moment was anything but funny.

"You're laughing at me?"

"No. I'm laughing because I feel so good. Don't you?" He kissed her neck, cuddling again, earning a soft giggle.

"I see your point." She joined in and collapsed in glee on top of him.

His laughter increased and they giggled like silly idiots. When their amusement died, she pushed herself up on one elbow and looked down at him. The desire mirrored in that heated gaze had him filling her. He couldn't stop his hands from plowing into those thick black tresses. He wound his fingers through silken strands and tugged, catching her lips with his. In moments, he was no longer in control as hips pumped of their own volition while she rode him with the skill of a seasoned lover. His every thrust was gripped tighter before he finally followed her into another explosive orgasm.

When Ñico could think again, he opened his eyes.

Pepper expelled a soft, breathy sigh before her head landed into that perfect spot on his shoulder. He was too sated to move. Legs and arms had turned into jelly. Still, he couldn't stop his arms from wrapping around her, while fingers mixed with locks of her hair slid soothingly up and down her arms because of this urge to touch her. For the longest time, he did nothing but stroke. Her skin felt so soft. So tender. Ñico sighed and closed his eyes. Thoughts of how he was going to tell her the truth about who he was infiltrated his consciousness. He pushed them out, unwilling to let anything mar the perfection of the night. He'd deal with the truth later. Much later.

Chapter 7

Pepper must have fallen asleep because the next thing she knew, Nick had picked her up and was carrying her toward the luxurious bathroom.

A dozen candles lit the darkened room, casting shadows over the walls. He moved to sit with her on the edge of the whirlpool tub. Steam rose out of the bubble-filled water, adding a sauna-like warmth to the room.

Confusion clouded her eyes and she glanced questioningly at him. Seeing nothing in his expression, she squirmed.

"What—?"

Nick's finger rested on her lips. "Shush. Don't think. Just feel," he whispered, pivoting while she sat in his lap. His thumb trailed back and forth, drawing a soft smile of contentment.

He planted his feet before slowly sinking with her into the steaming water. As his mouth lowered, her last rational thought was that she'd chosen well for her first time. Nick Guerrero was such a skilled lover.

His slow, languid kisses gave Pepper no choice but to obey his soft commands.

Don't think. Just feel.

This leisurely round of lovemaking wasn't the out-of-control sex they'd experienced earlier, but it was every bit as hot.

They thoroughly made use of his whirlpool bathtub, then drank wine and ate dinner on the terrace in candlelight before they made love again. For the rest of the night, she followed his edict to the letter. She felt everything and then some.

Much later, a ringing cell phone woke her. Pepper stretched and smiled, totally filled with…*ahhhh*…love and happiness and satisfaction. Though sore and slightly stiff, she felt satisfied, like someone who'd just enjoyed a rich, decadent meal. Memories of the wonderful night spent in Nick's arms rushed back. Dreamily staring at the ceiling, her smile deepened. Imagine being married to such a man! She never thought she was one of those who pictured herself wearing a white dress while escorted by her father down the aisle, but those thoughts wouldn't recede. She needed to call home. Hopefully, her dad would understand.

The same insistent tone that woke her broke into her blissful thoughts again. Her gaze flew to the nightstand beside the king-size bed. She reached for the annoying device and sat upright. She palmed it and peered down to check the caller ID. The ringing stopped.

She glanced at the bathroom door. Nick must be in the shower since she heard running water. Her attention returned to the phone. Why would her mother be calling? Intending to find out, she pressed the button to retrieve the message and brought the phone to her ear, as Elena's voice burst forth.

"Angelina? I'm calling to warn you. Antonio knows where you are. I think Ñico's on his way to woo you. Call me back as soon as you get this message. We need to talk."

"Ñico?" she murmured. A streak of uncertainty filled her. Her gaze flew to the bathroom door. It couldn't be, could it?

She saw Nick's cell phone on the dresser and picked it up. He had a voice mail. Mentally groaning, she worked the phone to retrieve his messages. The entire time she kept her attention on the closed door, her heartbeat soared out of control.

"Ñico? Miguel Delgado. Have you found your prize? Have you made contact? Elena is not too happy with me at this moment. Not since she found out I've been assisting you. Call me back. I have a feeling my wife will be warning my daughter, so I want to prepare you."

Ñico? Her stomach churned as an acid of realization erupted, eating into her satisfied soul. She closed her eyes, praying it wasn't what she thought. But she didn't believe in coincidences. There was no way her father would be calling a stranger.

She switched the phone off, then pushed the button again, waiting the never-ending seconds before the phone rebooted and flashed the words, "Hola, Antonio Fernández."

Antonio Fernández? The man her father had ordered her to marry?

Her heart sank. Despair and disillusionment completely replaced her earlier happiness, then in seconds, were themselves succeeded by anger.

Her fist clenched. Nails dug into her skin almost drawing blood until she felt pain and relaxed them somewhat.

How dare he!

Pepper jumped off the bed and ran to the bathroom door, flinging it open and shouting profanity in rapid-fire Spanish, words her mother would be mortified to hear from her lips. But damn it all, she could barely contain her fury.

She yanked the shower door open, startling one wet, naked hunk.

"What?" Nick said, his expression clearly adding to the question.

Nick…no, not Nick. Ñico turned off the water. Then, straightening in all his naked glory, complete with muscles flexing as drops of water trailed along the bronzed bulges, he stared at her, the surprised glimmer in his eyes turning more suggestive. As a distraction to keep from meeting his inviting gaze, her eyes lowered, focusing on a few drops heading toward his waist. As they got caught on the dark hair above his groin, she froze, forcing her gaze higher.

"Would you like to join me, *querida*?"

His words got her attention and she remembered why she was so angry.

"Don't you *querida* me." Despite being naked herself, she ignored his sexy grin. The grin that both knew could melt her insides. That smile could melt icebergs, it was so hot.

"You jerk," she hissed, continuing her diatribe of cursing him in Spanish, and ending with "Damn you, Ñico!" She pronounced his name, using the proper pronunciation, with the *N* pronounced like a *Y*, and held up his cell phone. "Imagine Antonio Fernández and Nick Guerrero being one and the same. You bastard!" She threw the phone at him as hard as she could and stalked out of the room, slamming the door behind her for effect.

She quickly started dressing, stepping into her shorts. Without doing the zipper, she reached for her shirt, but was grabbed from behind and thrown onto the bed. A dripping wet

Ñico followed, landing on top of her.

His actions only made her madder, if that were possible. Using her fists, she pummeled his chest, back, and arms trying to dislodge the immovable, two-hundred-pound mass of masculine muscles. He snatched her wrists, imprisoning her arms above her head. Beads of water dripped from his hair, a few trailing down her body, sending a trickle of sensation into her consciousness as her glance landed on his erection.

Pepper forced her attention higher, refusing to let the sight of him fully aroused affect her.

"It won't do you any good to struggle. I'm not releasing you until you listen to me."

"Why would I listen to you?" She bucked, then tried to knee him in the groin, hoping against hope she'd hit her mark so she could yank out of his grip. She might as well have saved her energy. He was too fast and too strong. Still she wasn't about to give up.

"You lied to me." Breathing heavily from her exertions, she looked him square in the eye and sneered, "Antonio."

"An omission I meant to rectify, *querida*."

"When? And I'm not your *querida*."

"Yes, you are."

"No, I'm not." She pushed again. "Will you get off me? You're obnoxious and I don't want you near me."

"That's not what you said last night." Ñico kissed her neck, moving to her ear, where he spent a long moment nibbling before whispering. "You loved having me on top of you then."

Mercy, his fullness was too close. Pleasure in the form of heat pooled in her center. She didn't want to feel the sensations, nor did she like the effect his sexy tone or lips had on her resistance. Pepper pulled her head away, in an effort to hold on to her anger. "That was before I knew who you really were. Let go of me. Now."

An amused chuckle was her only answer.

She thrashed about, working harder to break out of his hold.

"You're adorable when you're angry." He planted a kiss on her forehead, then lifted up and met her gaze, grinning. "This is a side I've never seen before. To steal your phrase, so Latin and sexy as hell."

Pepper bit back her frustration, trying to chill him with a look, too fearful her need for him would slip out if she didn't. Oh, how she wished she could shove his amusement down his throat. She struggled some more, but all she did was draw another chuckle that enraged her further, giving her anger to cling to. After all, anger worked much better for her cause than sexual awareness.

She pried one leg free, and using as much force as she could muster, she kneed him again, aiming for his groin. But Ñico moved too fast, obviously anticipating her reaction.

"Ah, ah, ah. Watch the family jewels. We'll want to have *bambinos* after we're married."

Before she knew what he was doing, he'd removed her shorts, leaving her naked. She tried to ignore his nakedness, the way her body responded to his lack of clothing, and the heat now swamping her center. Jerking her leg free, she kicked with more exertion, petrified that if he did what she thought he was thinking of doing—planting himself in between her legs, making it more difficult to kick him with any force—she be screwed, literally.

"Will you stop fighting and listen?"

"No!" She still attempted to kick, even as more heat shot through her system. "There is nothing you have to say that I want to hear."

"Please," Ñico whispered. "Is it really so bad to discover the man who means to marry you can do this?" He began caressing her arm with his free hand, settling his body between her legs, hampering her from kicking him again. Pepper groaned inwardly, recognizing the begging in his tone, in his fingers. She had no defense against them, especially when he nudged her with his erection, now right above her center. She couldn't stop herself from moving to bring it closer.

How did he do that so easily? Elicit this driving need…this hunger…with just his touch and his voice? She closed her eyes, filled with self-loathing, fighting the desire to have him enter her. He was so close and she wanted him so much. *No!* She squirmed. She had to hold on to her resolve. He was Antonio Fernández, the man her father had demanded she marry, the man who'd made her fall in love with him, and he'd lied to her. Tears streaked down her face as she realized the truth.

Her tears flowed faster as all the implications of her predicament set in. She was in humongous trouble, because all she wanted to do was return his kisses and touch him as he was touching her.

"Please, Angelina, I never meant to hurt you." As if he sensed her acquiescence, he released her wrists, his hand roaming, kneading, sliding down the length of her, yanking yearning from her body, from her soul. "Give me a chance to explain."

When Ñico brushed her tears with his fingertips and added his lips, kissing them, she had no will to push him away, instead pulled him closer. Heat flared as his mouth followed the trail his hand took. He swept strands of hair off her neck and massaged behind her ear, keeping the contact gentle, extracting more need.

"That's all I ask," he murmured, before his lips found hers.

His mouth was too tempting. In seconds, she stopped fighting and started stroking, touching and caressing his hard body in invitation. Ñico obviously didn't need to be asked twice. Her soft moans floated past her ears as he entered her. Though she hated herself for giving in to the pleasure spreading throughout her body, she couldn't stop from responding to what he made her feel.

Once the last bit of pleasure faded, reality crept in and Pepper shoved in another attempt to push him off her. "Move!"

Ñico propped himself on an elbow and gazed down at her, grinning. "Will you listen to me?"

"Will you get off me?" She quirked an eyebrow, tamping down her rising irritation. He didn't have to be so damned sexy.

"I will if you promise to hear me out without going all crazy."

"Deal."

He withdrew from her, rising and grabbing a box of tissues. After taking a few, he handed the box to her and sat on the edge of the bed.

Pepper couldn't fight the irritation that overcame her at his casual manner. "Will you put on some pants?"

Ñico chuckled, but did as she requested. While he stepped into his shorts, Pepper reached for her t-shirt, donning it in seconds, using the bit of material as a barrier to his blatant appeal.

Even with a pair of shorts covering his nakedness, he was simply irresistible.

Don't forget who he is. Her mind screamed the warning, pulling her back to reality. She'd spent a glorious night and few minutes this morning in the arms of Antonio Fernández.

He really was a gifted lover and she thanked God he'd been her first, but she had to remember the end result would only mean heartache for her. There was no way a man like Antonio would settle for a monogamous marriage. His reputation had preceded him.

"Okay. I'm listening." Sullenly, Pepper leaned against the pillows, crossing her arms and glaring at him. Though he'd given her another earth-shattering orgasm, she had to disengage—both physically and emotionally—and stick to the facts. This was the same man she'd gone to a great deal of trouble to avoid. "You wanted to talk, so talk." He'd already proven how weak she was. She blinked back tears. She wouldn't give him any more ammunition.

He walked toward her. "*Querida*, I'm sorry."

Her chin inched up and her eyes flashed anger. "Don't call me that," she hissed.

Ñico halted in midstride, searching and meeting her gaze, eyes locking as he pulled his thoughts together. He pulled a hand through his hair and began pacing. "I didn't lie to you, exactly."

She snorted. "What would you call it?"

"*Quer–*"

"Don't," she warned, cutting him off.

He stopped, eyeing her thoughtfully. "Okay. I admit I twisted the truth to my benefit and omitted a few facts. But I had no choice."

"You could have told me who you really were."

"Would you have given yourself to me if you'd known?"

"Hell, no!" This time it was Pepper's turn to jump off the bed. She hurried to the window, tossed her hair over her shoulder and crossed her arms, hugging them to her chest. She glanced out at the gorgeous view without really seeing it. "I spent four years avoiding you."

"It saddens me to hear you say such a thing."

"You can't be serious?" She turned back to him and gaped.

Ñico met her scornful stare without flinching and nodded. "*Si, mi pequeña ángel*," he whispered. "Especially after last night."

She swallowed hard and stared into the ebony depths of his eyes, unable to stop the thought that he was being sincere from forming. She shook off the sentiment and continued looking out the window. Suddenly she pivoted as questions surfaced. Her eyes narrowed, viewing him suspiciously. She wasn't about to fall for his seductive techniques again. "Why did you come after me?"

"The obvious reason. It's time for me to marry. And who else would I marry, but you?" His expression turned more earnest. "You're mine. Have been since we sealed our bargain." His eyebrows rose. "You do remember what you promised that day, don't you?"

He would bring that up. "Doesn't count," she lied. Of course she remembered. Pepper couldn't let the fact that he also remembered sway her. "I was nine years old and very impressionable."

"Age has no bearing on this. There was a connection between us." When she gave a derisive snort, Ñico's spine stiffened. "Are you denying our bond?" he ground out, clenching his jaw. "My memory isn't faulty, *querida*. You felt something, just as I did. It was in your eyes. The image is etched into my brain, as if it happened yesterday."

She shook her head, wishing she could ignore the truth of his words. But a hazy glimpse, a nine-year-old's memory of the boy she thought she'd loved, his hair falling in front of that youthful face as he'd knelt before her, proudly asking her to be his when the time came, stuck with her. She hadn't set eyes on him since that day, purposefully avoiding any and all negative rumors, unwilling to distort a child's picture of perfection. Yet, his adult imperfections had been too hard to ignore. A womanizer and a player, Antonio Fernández had given the gossip rags plenty of fodder while he'd lived in England. She had felt something back then, but after listening to her mother's accounts of his escapades, Pepper had become cynical and had accepted the reality of what her feelings would manifest. Unhappiness. Loving a man who couldn't love her enough to be faithful would only yield pain in the end. She'd be just like her mother.

"If you remember everything so vividly, you had a poor way of displaying your feelings over the years." Her chin notched higher, daring him to answer for his past deeds. "Did you think I'd never hear about all the women who preceded me?"

"I was young and stupid and vastly indiscreet." His hands went up in surrender. He flashed a sheepish grin, his expression giving him the look of an errant schoolboy found cheating. "And I've already told you that had more to do with gaining my *padré's* notice. I certainly hadn't been thinking of the day I would have to face you."

"Oh, yeah. Like you're planning on being faithful now?"

Ñico's grin died as he met her gaze squarely. "I will not dishonor you."

She stiffened, her eyes narrowing as she processed his answer. "What exactly does that mean?"

"We will be married. Have children. We'll be a family."

"But what about fidelity?"

"I'll be yours in what counts. My name and my holdings." He shrugged, his expression saying he couldn't promise more, but he didn't actually voice the words.

Pepper sighed and looked away, hiding her disappointment. So like him and the other males in her family. At least he was being honest, not promising something he couldn't deliver.

"For what it's worth," he whispered, gripping her shoulders, drawing her focus again. "I can truthfully tell you no one has ever caught my attention the way you have, both then and now."

Pepper shut her eyes tight, praying. Would it be enough to hold him, to keep him from straying?

"Don't say no yet. Come home to Isla del Diablo with me." The proud conquistador she noted earlier stood before her, his gaze begging. "What can it hurt to at least think about marriage to me? We have much in common and do well together in the bedroom. Give us a chance."

She wanted to, so damn much. Why did it have to be Antonio Fernández who held her heart? *What can it hurt*, he asks, and this from a man who could only end up hurting her.

"Don't you think it's time to stop running from who you

are?"

Pepper's back straightened. Using her annoyance as a crutch, she said, "I'm no longer running. I have a life here."

His eyebrows shot up. "A life?"

"Yes. Friends. People I care about." She began pacing again.

"Don't forget your old movies. They will definitely keep you warm on cool nights." Nico ignored the dirty look she shot him and walked over to the patio door, peering out, hands clasped behind his back, remaining silent. "What about children of your own? And family?" he finally asked.

She slanted a glance in his direction, noting his erect stance. Even half-dressed in shorts, he was an imposing, confident man.

He turned, catching her gaze, halting her. "You haven't seen yours since you've run. All that time without them has to be hard on you. As I recall, yours was a close-knit one."

"Your point?" It appeared he knew her well.

"No point. Just stating facts. And you have no love life." He smiled. "Or had none until I showed up."

Of course I didn't, she wanted to say. *I was waiting for you to show up and do just what you did. Sweep me off my feet. Only, I want you to love me always and never stray.* But she didn't vocalize that, either. Instead she offered, "I'm happy for the moment."

"If we married, I could make you happier, give you *bambinos.* Can you honestly say you don't want them, even if you lie to yourself about wanting me?"

Pepper didn't answer. Why bother when he spoke the truth? He did have the power to make her happy. She'd love to bear his children, and she did want him. But he'd also make her unhappy. Of that, she had no doubt.

"I want you for my wife. A choice I made so young is still my choice now." Nico took the few steps separating them. Smiling tenderly, he brushed a lock of hair off her face, securing it behind her ear. His fingers lingered and the back of his hand slid up and down her cheek in a soothing motion. "How about it, *querida?* Will you give us consideration?"

She bit her bottom lip as indecision flooded her mind. He was so tempting, staring at her with those dark, soul-searing eyes of his, his grave expression saying so much. She felt he actually did care for her.

Unable to hold his intent gaze any longer, Pepper looked down and studied the designs in the carpet, thinking. She had the means with one more week of her two-week vacation looming, could even take another week, if necessary. She hadn't seen her family in too long, adding more temptation. Plus it was time to face the past, face Ñico, and determine if she did, indeed, want to honor her promise. Problem was, she knew once she set on a path for home, her decision would be harder to make in the end. She rubbed her temples as more of the same thoughts filled her head.

Closing her eyes, she faced the brutal truth. Why fight it? Her choice had been made the minute they made love. More than anything, she desired to be his lady, and she could hold the job for the next two weeks if she went home with him. At this point, she'd follow him anywhere and endure the pain of separation later.

Chapter 8

The second the seat belt sign went out, Pepper jumped up and paced the small jet Ñico had rented to fly them to Isla del Diablo.

"Will you stop?" Ñico said, minutes later. "You're making me dizzy."

"I can't help it. I'm nervous. When I get nervous, I pace." She wiped her sweaty palms on her dress slacks, peered out the window, and saw only various shades of blue. The plane was now well over the ocean. She had an hour, or less, to stew before they landed.

Ñico reached across the aisle, his fingers wrapping around her arm. He gave a gentle tug. "Come here."

She landed on his lap.

"Why are you so distressed, *querida*," he whispered, nibbling on her ear, planting more kisses along her jaw as he brushed her hair aside. "You have nothing to worry about. They're your family and they love you."

"I've been thinking." Pepper shrugged. "You hit a nerve earlier when you said I should never have run." She pressed nonexistent wrinkles out of her slacks, not meeting his glance. "I'm worried about facing Papa. I should've had the guts to confront him four years ago and tell him I'd decided against marriage to you. I didn't, and now have to face the fact that I disappointed him." She didn't add that he'd disappointed her by straying outside his marriage. Yet she'd forgiven him. Her mother had chastised her for making judgments, and Pepper finally realized, if Elena could live with his indiscretions, who was she to judge? After all, their marriage was their private business and none of her concern. Would her father view this situation in the same way? Or would he judge her and try to control her as he'd done before?

"I figured you and your father were close, but I didn't realize until now how close you must have been."

"We were at one time." She forced a sad smile. "I was his little girl and only his best friend's son was good enough for me." Her shoulders went up, and her smile turned self-deprecating. "I snubbed my nose at his choice and ran away from both of you."

"You're underestimating him. Give him the chance to show how much he cares. I'll make sure he knows this is your decision and give him the parameters of our agreement."

Nodding, Pepper expelled a deep breath. She'd told Ñico she needed to review her decision and he'd receive his answer regarding marriage in two weeks. Two weeks' time to decide her destiny. To decide if she could live with the knowledge and dread of discerning at some point her heart would be ripped out of her chest when Ñico no longer thought of her as *his lady*. Oh, she could have his name and bear his children, but did she stand the chance of ever owning his heart as he did hers? The thought of him doing with another woman what they'd done the last two nights ate at her soul.

Sighing heavily, she stared out the window. Why torture herself wanting something she'd never have?

"Don't fret, *querida*." His hand covered hers and squeezed.

The sexy, confident grin Ñico presented had the butterflies fluttering, turning her stomach into a quivering mess.

"We'll work it out."

Pepper returned his smile and nodded. If only it could be so easy. If only they could work it out. If only he'd be satisfied with her for a lifetime, then she'd be the happiest person on the planet.

"Your friends seemed delighted by your news."

"I guess they're just romantics at heart," she said, thinking of Rachel and Karen's reactions when she told them of her past and why she'd be taking off more than two weeks. Both seemed to grasp the momentous decision confronting her, telling her not to worry, despite not knowing the full facts of her dilemma. She leaned back in the seat remembering Rachel's plea. "You determine what's best for you. That's what Second Chances is all about. Twisting fate to create second chances at life."

Neither friend knew how much she prayed for this second chance at love. How she wanted this opportunity to twist fate.

~

"Pepper!" Elena Delgado's voice produced tears of joy.

Pepper's speed increased. Without having to deal with security at the private airfield both families were members of, her parents were waiting on the tarmac when she stepped off the jet once it landed. By the time she reached them, she was running.

"Mama." She wrapped her arms around her mother and squeezed her fiercely. Oh, how she'd missed her parents. Until this moment she hadn't realize how much.

"How is my Peppita?" Miguel Delgado asked, when she pulled away from her mother and stepped back.

"Oh, Papa!" Blinking back more tears, Pepper fell into his outstretched arms, hugging him as tightly as he hugged her. Maybe Ñico was right about her underestimating his love after all. "I'm fine."

"Pepper? Peppita?" Grinning, Ñico came up behind her. His eyebrows rose a good inch. "I thought the name was an alias."

"No. The name means something," Pepper explained, unable to hold on to her giggle because her father's grin said he remembered. "I couldn't quite shed my complete past when I moved away. As silly as it seems, it somehow kept me connected to home."

"I had a hunch she might keep her nickname, which paid off. It's how I found her in the Florida Keys." Miguel clapped Ñico on the back and took his offered hand. "Pepper is what I started calling her after she put the stuff in my coffee one morning. She couldn't have been more than ten or eleven at the time." He laughed. "Got my attention, I'll tell you. But then, she's always spiced up my life, always kept things lively. It seemed a fitting moniker, as I was always wondering what she'd do next."

"I can see not much has changed."

"I'd be disappointed if it had." Miguel stood proudly, his fists on his hips, studying his daughter. "Did you think I was jesting when I told you she was a handful?"

"Papa!" Pepper felt the rush of heat sliding up her face. How embarrassing to be caught in the middle while they talked as if she wasn't present.

Nico chuckled and kissed her cheek. "I'm glad I listened."

"I had no doubt you could handle her." Miguel shook his head grinning, and stepped in between Nico and her, his arms encircling both before herding the group toward the parked limousine.

The driver emerged and opened the doors at their approach.

"So, when is the wedding? You two make a beautiful couple. Together, you'll make beautiful grandchildren." Miguel lowered his arms, releasing them, and halted in front of the car, eyeing first Pepper, then Nico, apparently waiting for an answer.

Pepper's worried gaze flew to Nico's.

He grinned, giving her a meaningful wink, clearly saying, *I've got it covered*, before turning to Miguel. "We haven't set a date yet."

"Better hurry." Miguel grunted, his smile fading. "Paulo and I have waited too long already. Your *padré* won't live forever. Plus, Elena and I aren't getting any younger. We want grandchildren and before we get them, she's apt to change her mind again."

The elder Delgado assisted his wife into the limo, then turned to Pepper, offering his hand.

"Open your eyes," he murmured, halting her when she tried to scurry past him. "Antonio Fernández is a prize catch. The perfect match for you. Surely you see that, Peppita?"

Pepper bristled at her father's autocratic tone. Now she remembered why she'd hidden in the Florida Keys for four years. Nico hadn't been the only man she'd been running from. She brushed past her father, sliding into the opposite seat, as Miguel added, "Don't let this opportunity get away."

Nico climbed in beside her, gripped her knee, and squeezed. "Don't worry, *querida*. I'll keep my promise," he whispered. "It is your decision, not his." Then his gaze met hers and he flashed his sexy grin. "But I'll be doing my damnedest to make you see things my way." His smile turned smug. "I am a prize catch, though. More than that, I am your perfect match."

~

"So, is she as beautiful as her mother?" Paulo Fernández asked, leaning back studying him.

Holding eye contact, Nico nodded. "More, if that's possible."

His gaze lowered. A smile crossed his face, as thoughts of Pepper and their lovemaking swirled inside his brain. His smile deepened. He'd always rated his sex life as sizzling, definitely better than average, especially after sleeping with some of the sexiest women in the world over the years. But nothing in his past encounters could compare with making love with his wild angel that first night. And it just kept getting better.

His father cleared his throat, pulling him out of his pleasant thoughts and on to the more distasteful task facing him. His smile died. He sat trapped in a plush chair in front of Paulo's mahogany desk, not particularly pleased to be here, but knowing the old man wouldn't be content until he got what he wanted from this inquisition.

He focused on Paulo's stern face and caught remnants of his dead brother. However, unlike Juan, who'd always been Ñico's champion, the elder Fernández constantly scrutinized his life, and Ñico never failed to come up lacking under such intense examination.

"Is a wedding imminent?"

"In due time." Ñico wasn't inclined to expand on his answer, unwilling to give Paulo any tidbit to pick apart in his dealings with Pepper. Their relationship was personal and not open for discussion. "Pepper Delgado is not an easy woman to convince."

"Then you're not working hard enough. Despite being your mother's son, I'll never believe a man with your persuasive charm can't be convincing. It's a Fernández trait."

Ñico flinched inwardly. The smile he offered his father wasn't genuine. "She came home with me, didn't she? I just need time with her." The Delgados had invited him to dinner and were giving him plenty of latitude in managing their daughter. Why couldn't his father see that? Paulo would never change. He and his sisters did favor their mother in looks. Which was something Ñico had determined long ago played a big part in why he'd always been the out-of-favor second son. "Charm or no charm, I can't push too hard. She's still a little wary of overbearing men."

"I hear she's quite the pistol." Paulo chuckled. "You don't want a woman who has no backbone. I'm telling you, Delgado's daughter is the perfect match for my son. But you'd better hurry.

I'm not getting any younger and I want to see a grandson before I die."

Ñico mentally snorted. Of course he did. Yet Paulo still looked young and vital, certainly not like someone with cancer or the sixty-five years of his last birthday, and he'd probably outlive everyone around him, even with a manageable disease.

"Don't worry, Papa," Ñico murmured. "We'll be married. As soon as I can arrange it."

Ñico's plans were falling into place. He'd seduced Pepper. At this point, she yearned for his touch as much as he yearned for hers. But over the course of the last twenty-four hours, he'd decided it wasn't enough. He now wanted Pepper to enter into their marriage with the same intensity she'd displayed when they'd made love.

Willingly and without uncertainty.

The idea didn't make sense to him, but it tugged at him nonetheless.

He'd definitely lost ground when he'd skirted the issue of fidelity. There'd been no doubt in his mind Pepper had grasped the meaning of his omission and hesitation. More than anything, he'd wanted to allay her fears and comfort her. Tell her he'd never stray. Yet, how could he promise something he didn't deem possible? He'd had no choice other than to outright lie, and that he wouldn't do. If they were to live together in harmony, they'd have to deal honestly with each other, and she'd have to accept him as he was. A Fernández male with a voracious appetite for passion.

"I've waited too long for this." Paulo rubbed his hands together, drawing Ñico out of his musings. His father grinned, his expression mirroring his statement. "Your assurance pleases me. Very much."

Ñico nodded, thankful to finally have done something to please the overbearing man. The inquisition was nearly over. Now if he could figure out a way to please Pepper and get her to marry him as he'd promised his father and in a manner that would please himself, his life would be perfect.

~

"You aren't going soft on her, are you?"

85

"Why do you ask?" Ñico took the Scotch on the rocks Miguel Delgado offered after being led into his office. Having just endured the meeting with his own father, he wasn't in the mood to placate. He sat, keeping all emotion off his face. Bringing the glass to his lips, he sipped, eyeing the older man. His interference was unnecessary and unwanted. Though he owed Delgado for the information on Pepper's whereabouts, his business with her was now just that. His business.

"What's this we haven't set a date yet? I know a diversionary tactic when I hear it. I told you how to go after her, and now that victory is within your reach, you're stalling." Delgado swirled the amber liquid in his glass, staring at it thoughtfully. Then he looked up and met Ñico's gaze, his eyes reflecting concern. "Why?"

"I have my reasons. I'm handling the situation." Swallowing his irritation, Ñico chuckled, presenting an amused countenance when amusement was the furthest thing from his thoughts. "I know how to deal with Pepper. She has to think the choice is hers, otherwise she'll balk."

Delgado huffed. "That's the whole point. Of course she'll balk. She's always balked. But marriage to you is her duty. Did you tell her that?"

"I see it worked for you four years ago." Ñico shrugged. "As I'm sure you reminded her before she disappeared."

"That was her mother's doing." Delgado waved off the comment in disgust, before leaning forward and pointing an accusing finger at him. "Besides, if you'd kept a lid on your activities, we wouldn't be having this conversation."

Ñico stiffened. He stilled his body and spoke carefully. "Pepper will do her duty. After all, I got her here to Isla del Diablo, didn't I?"

His comment seemed to satisfy the older man. Delgado remained silent before shaking his head and saying, "I love her dearly, but I'll never understand her." He sighed heavily and drank a deep gulp from his glass. "She became so feisty and combative as she grew into an adult. By the time she ran away, my sweet Pepper had developed quite a kick."

"Don't worry, Miguel. I understand her need to assert her independence."

"She favors Elena, but Elena was always more predictable and not as stubborn." He grunted, brandishing a negligent wave. "Kids. They never act the way you think they should." He took another sip and leaned back, crossing one leg over the other before his gaze settled sharply on Ñico. "Exactly how do you aim to curb this independent streak? You have to know it's not conducive to a good marriage."

It's none of your concern, Ñico wanted to shout. He loved her independence, enjoyed sparring with her feisty and combative personality. Instead of relaying his thoughts, he inhaled deeply, biting his tongue. Miguel Delgado was as tenacious as his own father, and Ñico realized Delgado wouldn't give up until he got what he wanted. *Dios* save him from interfering old men. In an effort to shut him up, he offered, "Once she has children, she'll change her focus."

They hadn't used protection, and since he doubted a virgin would be on the pill, he was hoping she might already be pregnant. If not, he'd keep trying. A *bambino* would solidify his position in her life. And, contrary to Delgado's belief, he hadn't gone soft. In fact, Ñico's determination grew stronger. He'd discovered having Pepper for his wife had become as necessary as breathing.

Ñico hesitated before throwing out his ace. "There's the possibility she's pregnant now."

Delgado stiffened. "The news is not particularly something a father likes to hear. If you had been any other man making this revelation, you'd be a dead one." His thunderous expression and tone added to his threat. "And such news is all the more reason not to delay your wedding."

"I told you, I'm handling it." Ñico wasn't intimidated. At this point, he was more worried about gaining Pepper's full compliance than his future father-in-law's wrath. This need to have her willingly accept what was between them drove him.

"While you're handling it, handle this," Delgado said, his voice still menacing. "Since you've already had the honeymoon, I expect a wedding. Soon."

"I don't believe this," Pepper yelled, throwing her hands in the air, as the object of their conversation burst into the room just then, throwing out her chest in indignant fury, drawing both men's attention. Recognizing a regal Spanish queen ready to do battle, Ñico swore under his breath.

"Once I have children? I'll change my focus? And what focus would that be?" She caught his gaze, her condemning glare all but wilting him with its intensity, her haughty head held high. "I hope you don't expect me to roll over and play dead if we marry. Because I've got news for you, *querida*," she said, sneering the endearment. "If we *ever* marry, I plan on keeping my independence."

"You shouldn't eavesdrop." Ñico cleared his throat, feeling the noose wrap around his neck.

"Pepper." Delgado nodded. "Ñico's right. We were having a private conversation. "

She turned on her father, her back straightening. "One that included me, which is why I felt compelled to hear what you had to say."

"It's okay, Miguel. I'll handle things. This is between Pepper and me."

"And why should I listen to you?" She spun around quickly, all but pouncing on him in a verbal attack. "'Give him the chance to show how much he cares. I'll make sure he knows this is your decision and give him the parameters of our agreement.' Those were your exact words. Yet, I don't believe you mentioned anything along those lines in the last few minutes." Her chin went up a notch. "All I heard was the two of you discussing me as if I were a piece of chattel with no brain or will of my own."

"You misunderstood." Ñico stood and strolled toward her, then met her blistering gaze without flinching and smiled, hoping he could smooth over his idiocy. "If you come in at the tail end, you miss vital parts that have already been discussed." Pepper had obviously overheard part of their conversation and he could only imagine how it had come across. At the moment, he could kick Delgado for his stupidity. The old man should have kept his mouth shut and had the good sense to realize that Ñico had the situation well in hand. Now, he had to back up and do damage control.

"Oh?" Pepper's eyebrows shot up. "What vital points did I misunderstand?" She held out a hand and started counting. "Papa was concerned because he thought you were going soft, using diversionary tactics, I think was how he worded it, and you replied that you know how to deal with me. In fact, you're handling me. That about sums it up." She put up her other hand. "No, wait. Let's not forget your way of handling me is to get me pregnant and Papa expects a wedding because we've already had the honeymoon." Their gazes locked. "Did I miss anything?"

"It's not what you think."

"Then please enlighten me." Eyes wide as quarters, she crossed her arms, tapping her foot.

He studied her thoughtfully, remaining silent. Judging by the steely glint in her eyes, smoothing over his stupidity with mere words wouldn't be an easy task. He groaned inwardly. He was so screwed. He now had a greater appreciation for the fitting American vernacular.

"Well?" she said. "I'm waiting."

Ñico sighed and rubbed his face with his hand, working to keep the growing annoyance he felt in check. "I was speaking privately with your father and had no idea you were listening. If I had, I wouldn't have spoken so bluntly."

"Which doesn't ease my mind any."

"Enough!" Delgado's voice boomed behind him, startling them both. "You gave yourself to him. There is nothing else to discuss."

"So that's what this is about?" Pepper met her father's livid stare, hers spitting fire. "I'm expected to marry because we spent the night together?"

"Why did you come home if not to fulfill your duty and marry?" Delgado replied, his voice just as hot and angry as hers.

Weaker men would cringe under such fire on both sides. Expecting no less from his wildcat with her claws unsheathed, Ñico stifled a smile. Marriage to his wild angel would never be boring. Despite his gargantuan task of redirecting her passion, aiming it toward lovemaking rather than fighting against him due to his error in judgment, he relished the challenge of taming her.

"I came home to decide what I wanted, not to fulfill my duty!"

"Sleeping with him tells me you made your choice, one you

made long ago, I might add. And I'm holding you to that choice."

"I was nine years old. Plus, this is the twenty-first century." Pepper stomped her foot as she ground out, "Get this straight, both of you. If and when I marry, it will be my choice as an adult woman. Just because we spent the night together isn't enough of a reason to marry." She caught Ñico's gaze, searing him with a stare that shouted her sincerity, and poked his chest, almost pushing him back with her finger's vehemence. "FYI, I don't need to be married to bear children. Women no longer have a negative stigma if they are single mothers. I'm a wealthy woman with the means to care for any child I conceive. Even one of yours." Once she hurled her impassioned avowals, she stomped out of the room.

"No daughter of mine will bear bastards, you hear me," Delgado yelled to her departing back. He turned and demanded, "Go after her! Make her see her duty."

"Miguel, you're not helping matters." Ñico rolled his eyes heavenward, swearing under his breath. The old man just had to prod the smoking fire of Pepper's irritation, creating an even bigger problem.

"You have to take the bull of my daughter's stubbornness by the horns, Ñico, otherwise she'll walk all over you."

Ñico bit back a nasty retort, holding on to his temper. Rather than saying what he really thought, he went for diplomacy instead. "Pepper has been on her own for too long to listen to anything you or I _tell_ her. I'll handle this in my own way, if you don't mind."

"I expect no less than marriage, especially after your admission."

"I understand what you expect." He polished off the rest of the Scotch. The heat of the liquid slid down his throat, easing some of the tension he felt. He slammed the glass on the table and turned, allowing the seriousness of what he was about to impart show in his eyes. "Now I'm telling you—the subject of our marriage is between Pepper and me and is no longer your concern. I'll thank you to keep out of it from now on." He should have told him that to begin with. Then, he wouldn't be in this mess.

"Your father will not be pleased."

"I'm sure you're going to enlighten him." Ñico stared at the older man, then shook his head, curling his lip in disgust. Of course Delgado would talk to his father. The two men were too much alike for him to see any other outcome. Now he'd have to placate not only Pepper, but Paulo Fernández as well. He turned and stalked out of the room as Delgado's "I only hope you know what you're doing," followed him.

Chapter 9

Pepper stormed off, heading for the ocean's edge by way of the trail she'd always used before her escape from the island all those years ago. Her parents' house was situated on a bluff, a perfect spot to capture both the water's breezes and the breathtaking view. Yet Pepper ignored the beauty in front of her, too annoyed to notice anything but her own fury. Despite the earlier joy her reunion brought on, now all she could think of was why she'd left in the first place.

When her feet hit the sand, she took a few more steps before taking off her sandals, dropping them, then kept going until clear water lapped at her toes. At that point, she turned and continued her ambling, using the time to think.

Oh, how she wished she hadn't been standing outside her father's library. Hadn't heard what she had. Ignorance was bliss, because this searing pain inside her heart made her realize it was a prelude to what her life would be like if she married Ñico.

"There you are. I've been looking for you."

Startled out of her thoughts, she turned toward her brother's voice. She'd been so swathed in misery she hadn't detected his approach. Shading her eyes from the sun, she took in Felipe Delgado, noting an imposing, handsome man with dark features, so like her father and Ñico. But unlike them, he had a fiery temperament similar to hers. Her brother, the artist, was barefoot. As he sauntered closer, she took in his faded jeans and ratty, paint-streaked t-shirt, which meant he'd been working in his studio. The errant lock of black hair falling over one eyebrow completed the petulant-little-boy look women seemed to find irresistible.

"What's the matter? Don't you remember me?" Tsk-tsking, he continued walking until he stood two feet in front of her. With arms spread wide, Felipe grinned. "I realize I was self-absorbed in creating when you got here. But I deserve more than a blank look after so long, don't you think?"

"Oh, Felipe!" Offering a genuine smile, Pepper didn't hesitate to close the remaining gap. The rest of her irritation faded as he engulfed her in a big bear hug. She couldn't hold on to the giggle that snuck forth. "I'm sorry. I was thinking and you surprised me."

"I missed you, Pep-squeak." He released her and affectionately tugged her ponytail, something he used to do to irritate her before her disappearance. "I'm glad you've come to your senses and are back home where you belong."

"I missed you. It feels good to be here." Ignoring his little dig, she nodded at his attire. "I see you're still painting. Your name is a buzzword in the Key West art circle these days, from what I hear." Growing up, they'd been inseparable. Though Felipe was two years older, he'd always had time for his little sister, allowing her to tag along with him until he went away to school, attending the Art Institute of Chicago. Then, while she'd been in college, he'd tried to control her life from a distance in his typical, male Delgado style, becoming an overbearing protector she hadn't felt she'd needed. They'd drifted further apart, mainly because Pepper had formed her own opinions, which hadn't meshed with his, causing many heated debates in the last year she'd lived on the island. Still, when Pepper had departed, leaving him had felt like chopping off an arm.

"I'm making my mark," he said, answering her question and giving her hair another tug. "Few truly understand my genius, though."

"Genius is rarely understood." Pepper laughed when the free-spirited brother of her youth flashed a mouthful of white teeth. Suddenly, the years as well as their old arguments fell away.

"Hmmm. Guess not." Felipe's narrow-eyed gaze scrutinized her face before it swept the landscape. "So, what's going on? How come you're down here and not up there with your fiancé?"

Pepper's focus followed his hand. Nico stood at the top of the bluff, staring back.

"Same old, same old," she said, unwilling to delve into her love life with her brother and destroy their brief truce. She knew perfectly well his chauvinistic views. They'd argued too many times before she left for her to believe he'd had a sudden change of heart. According to Felipe, men were put on this earth to conquer, whether they battled women in the bedroom or men in the boardroom. He was the consummate warrior, despite wielding a paintbrush as his weapon of choice.

"I don't understand. He's obviously here to see you, and you came home with him. Why are you now avoiding him?"

"Please, don't start." Pepper sighed and began walking. He followed, easily keeping her brisk pace. "I will not be controlled. This is an old argument and one I don't want to get into. Let's just agree to disagree."

"I see." Her brother stopped and grabbed on to her arm, halting her. "Which can only mean one thing. You're still holding on to your foolhardy viewpoint on how men should be?"

"It's not foolhardy. It's how I feel. Men view women as equals and are monogamous in the States. You're living in the past if you think women will put up with husbands who have to control and can't remain faithful. Look at our parents! They're a perfect example of what happens."

"Just because it worked out for Mama with Papa, doesn't mean all men can be as accommodating."

"What do you mean?" Her eyebrows furrowed and she studied his face. "Isn't their marriage now one of convenience?"

"Is that what she told you?"

"No." Pepper shook her head, more confused than ever. "Mama never mentioned the unhappy details in her letters and I've never asked, unwilling to know them."

"There are no unhappy details to learn. Their union remains a happy one."

"Really?"

"Yes." Felipe sighed, offering a sad smile. "But don't go painting Papa a romantic soul. He had no choice. When Mama threatened to leave, he caved and changed his ways, but there was more behind his decision than what you'd consider as love."

"I didn't know. Why did she never tell me?"

"I have no idea." He met her gaze with a fervent stare. "It doesn't alter the facts as I see them. A woman's job is to serve her man and remain faithful. But a man's role is different. We're providers and protectors, and as such, men roam." He shrugged, his expression adding to the simplicity of his statement. "It's not in our nature to stay monogamous."

"But you just said Papa changed. If he did, then so can others," Pepper said, as hope filled her. She would not let her brother's viewpoint and attitude dissuade her from being optimistic.

"It's not what you think." Felipe snorted, shaking his head. "His change of heart had more to do with time and energy. Papa's getting on in years, and his libido most likely slowed, so it was no great sacrifice."

Her hope died a quick death. Felipe's explanation was probably closer to the truth. After all, Papa was her brother's role model, the main source of his ideas. And hadn't she heard her father urging Ñico, saying he was getting soft? He hadn't changed a bit.

Pepper pushed the unwanted thoughts aside and continued walking along the beach.

"You never answered my question." Felipe fell into step next to her. "Why are you down here and your fiancé's up there?" he asked, nodding behind him, indicating the bluff Ñico still occupied.

"I shouldn't have come home. I realize that now. I'm long past the age of being a puppet." She glanced back, then heaved a heavy sigh. "Papa thinks he can still control my life. I overheard him coaching Ñico on how to handle me. I'm being passed from one man to another. I interrupted and informed them I'm not so easily controlled." Her shoulders lifted in a slight shrug and she kicked the sand in front of her. "Now we're at an impasse as to *my* future."

"Papa's only doing what he thinks is right. And he has a point."

"Oh? And what point would that be? That I'm chattel and just supposed to roll over and not have an opinion and not expect fidelity? Apparently Ñico is to take over control. But I'm my own person now. I'll not live under any man's rule."

"Always ready to fight, aren't you." Her brother laughed, but there was nothing humorous in the quick burst. "Grow up, Pepper. This is the real world, dealing with real men, men of power. We aren't like everyone else. Ñico is one of us. If you don't marry him, you'll be making a big mistake."

"This coming from a man and one who has no idea what women want."

Felipe pulled out his cell phone and pushed the button to bring up the stored numbers, shoving it under her face. "I know what women want. This is full of women who've let me know exactly what they want. Each one would give their eyeteeth to prove it by marrying me without my promise of fidelity. And I can assure you, not one of them has any concern as to whether or not I'm controlling."

"What about love?"

"That's an illusion, Pep-squeak." He shook his head, sighing out a long exhale. "The best you can do is to marry someone of your class. Someone who understands your role as an heiress. In my eyes, Antonio Fernández is that someone." He studied her for a moment. "Did any of those monogamous men you mentioned capture your attention? And if they did, did you tell them the total truth? Did they know about your money?"

Pepper didn't reply, unwilling to let him know how lonely her life in Florida had really been. She hadn't even realized how much, until Ñico showed up to highlight exactly what she'd been missing. How pathetic Felipe would find her if he knew she'd spent so much time idolizing dead men. How had she ever been content with watching old movies?

Ñico did seem to understand her and he had filled a void she'd never known existed. Would it be enough to last a lifetime without fidelity? Without his love?

"His father is urging this union, along with Papa, but it's obvious he has his own motivations."

"Ñico's father?" Pepper's focus landed on Ñico once more, discerning exactly what Felipe's words meant. She vaguely remembered Ñico mentioning trying to gain his *padré's* favor. Was that why he pushed so hard for her to marry him? The idea left her more unsettled.

"Use your brains!" Felipe grabbed her shoulders, giving a

gentle shake, his earnest expression adding to his chiding. "Use the body God gave you. You have much more influence than you think, and it has nothing to do with love and nothing to do with duty."

When her eyes narrowed in confusion, he snorted.

"He's taken with you, that much is obvious, even from this distance." Felipe spent a moment scrutinizing her face. "Are you still in love with him?"

She stiffened. "What do you mean?"

"You know exactly what I mean. Antonio Fernández was all you talked about at one time."

"That was years ago." Pepper felt heat rise up, as the idea of Felipe discovering how much she was taken with Ñico now flitted into her mind. She cast her gaze at the sand for a moment for fear he'd see the truth reflected in her eyes.

When she looked back up, he grinned. "Just as I suspected. The feeling's mutual. Use it. He may stray, but he'll always come home to you. He'll always protect you. It's our way, Pep-squeak. Accept it."

"So, tell me about your latest project," she said, in an effort to change the topic of their depressing conversation. She didn't want to think of Ñico straying, ever. "Any new shows coming up?"

"As a matter of fact…" While he droned on about his next showing in Miami six months from now, she locked arms with his and started walking, listening with only half an ear. The entire time her heart ripped in two.

~

"About time you joined us. We don't see you in almost four years and you disappear in a fit of anger," Miguel said to Pepper as she entered the dining room later that night. "Are you over your snit?"

Ñico watched the play of expressions cross her face, changing from surprise to irritation to acceptance.

She shrugged her shoulders. "I have to eat."

"Still sulking, I see." Miguel rolled his eyes, muttering a few not so nice words in Spanish.

"*Buenos noches, mi hija.* You look lovely tonight, Angelina."

Elena's words broke the tension between father and daughter. "I'm glad you could join us."

"You do look lovely, Pepper," Felipe said, coming in behind her. "As always."

Pepper held out her cheek for his brotherly kiss, then offered her mother a slight bow before gliding toward the table. Dressed elegantly in a long bronze gown accentuating her graceful and lithe body, with her glorious hair swept up in a fancy concoction held in place with a jeweled clip, she looked like a regal Spanish queen who deigned to break bread with the peasants.

When Ñico jumped up to pull out her chair, she sat beside him, not acknowledging his effort or his presence with so much as a look or a nod. His heiress picked up her water glass and took a large sip, keeping her gaze fastened in front of her. Then she shook out the napkin beside her and placed it on her lap, ignoring him as if he didn't exist.

Clenching and unclenching his fist, Ñico swallowed his annoyance and sighed.

Her actions told him he definitely had more work ahead of him than he'd originally thought. He'd waited for her to return from her walk, but after an hour with only her brother striding back along the sand as a result, he'd given up and decided to wait until later. Only later, which turned into now, didn't seem any better.

A servant arrived with a tray filled with *ensaladas*, and began working his way around the table.

While he served the salad, Ñico used the distraction, turning to Pepper. "Can we talk?"

His whispered voice drew her attention.

"Of course. We're considering marriage. Why wouldn't we talk?" She gave him a brilliant smile, only the warmth didn't reach her eyes.

He placed his hand on top of hers, and squeezed. "I had my reasons for saying such things, *querida*."

"I'm sure you did." Her back was as stiff as her voice.

When she tried to pull her fingers free, he tightened his hold in an effort to provoke, eyeing her intently. Quite tired of being invisible, he wasn't inclined to withstand her disinterest any longer.

"May I have my hand back?" Her chin notched up, her hot eyes daring him.

He grinned, locking gazes, and brought her hand to his lips, inciting a darker, more withering stare. Lesser men would squirm under her scathing expression. But not him. He enjoyed her reactions. He enjoyed taming her. His grin stretched. *Sí*, his feisty wildcat with her sharp little claws didn't disappoint him. Oh, how he relished the challenge of making her purr with contentment.

He turned her hand palm side up and kissed her wrist. Ñico held on to her gaze and made love with her hand, using strong fingers to rub, circling with his mouth and tongue, without curbing the desire he felt for her from reflecting in his eyes.

Pepper swallowed hard. A streak of pink highlighted her cheeks. Then she cleared her throat and he caught the glint in her eyes, as her rigid back straightened almost to the point of snapping in two.

"Are you quite done?" Her eyes narrowed and though she tried to conceal her emotions behind a condescending glare, he'd seen the sparks of what she couldn't hide. Desire. Want. Need.

"No, *querida*." Ñico lowered her hand, releasing his hold. "This is not over. If you think you can subdue my efforts with a scowl, you should rethink."

"I see." Her hand hastily retreated out of his reach to rest on her lap. "And what do you hope to gain with your *efforts*?"

He flashed a smug smile. "I've already gained it."

"Oh?" She quirked a brow. Her Royal Highness was back, enchanting him.

"*Sí, mi pequeña ángel*," Ñico said softly, his grin spreading. "I have."

Tonight he'd show his little angel exactly what he meant. If there was one thing he was good at, it was making women moan. Two nights spent in pure bliss with Pepper had already proven she wasn't immune to his lovemaking. He had no intention of slowing now. She would be pregnant with his babe soon and he shared Delgado's sentiments. No offspring of his would be born a bastard. He'd make damn sure of it.

"So, Pepper, how are the friends you mentioned in your letters? Karen and Rachel, I believe are their names?" Elena's voice cut through their play, pulling both his and Pepper's attention. "I'd enjoy hearing about your life in the Keys. I'm sure Miguel will, too."

Elena touched her husband's hand, sending a silent message, one Ñico hoped meant *Keep out of it.*

"Yes, Pepper." Ñico's eyebrows rose and he leaned back with interest, nodding to the servant who placed first his salad in front of him before placing Pepper's bowl on the table. "I'm sure they'll find your activities fascinating." He caught another one of her fuming glares and chuckled.

"I'd like to hear more about these friends," Felipe said. "I assume they're attractive?"

Dismissing him as if Ñico deserved no more thought, Pepper turned her focus to her brother and smiled. "My partners are both attractive, and because they are my friends I'm glad you live here and not there."

Felipe's hands crossed over his heart. "You wound me, Pep-squeak." But his grin belied the sentiment.

Pepper laughed and spent the next half hour recounting an active life with friends while living in the Florida Keys, not once sparing Ñico a glance. And though she did her best to ignore him during the meal, Ñico refused to allow the woman sitting next to him remain aloof and disinterested. His ego wouldn't allow her unspoken challenge to go unheeded. Not when he garnered such satisfaction from viewing how his *efforts* affected her.

Chapter 10

"I've got work to do." Felipe pushed away from the table. "I'll be in my studio." He bent to kiss Elena, then kissed Pepper and winked. "It is good to have you home. Isla del Diablo is where you belong, not some Florida key in America." He nodded to his father and Ñico, before heading for the door.

"If you will excuse me." Pepper stood, using her brother's timely exit for her own purposes. "I enjoyed the wonderful meal, but I'm tired. I think it's time I said good night."

"Of course, Angelina." Elena smiled. "Felipe has a point. I'm so happy to have you home where you belong."

Miguel grunted. "You've made us both happy. I'd be happier if you decided to take your duty more seriously."

Pepper ignored his taunt, never so relieved to have a meal finally come to an end in order to escape the man next to her. If she could just make it to her suite of rooms, she'd be okay.

Unfortunately, Ñico was quick to stand and offer his help. Pushing her chair under the table, he brushed the back of his hand against her breasts, causing them to tingle. That, along with the secret signals he'd kept sending with his eyes, not to mention his taunting innuendos during the meal, unnerved her.

"*Gracias*," she murmured, holding on to her temper. Mercy, would he simply leave her alone and let her breathe? She hurried in the direction of the hallway. Her irritation rose when she realized he'd followed on her heels, not giving her the space she craved.

"What is your problem?" she hissed, yanking out of his grasp after he'd placed a negligent arm around her in a proprietary move.

"I have no problem, *querida*." Leaning in close, he whispered so only she could hear, "But I do wish to speak with you in private."

The disdain-filled glance she spared him did nothing to

hinder Ñico's determination. His arm was back, steering her toward the patio door leading to the deck overlooking the water. The view of the moonlit ocean, as well as the dark setting, was just a little too romantic for her purposes, which had fast become a driving need to flee. She had no intention of being caught again in his amorous trap.

"This is far enough," she said, when they stopped at the gate, the top of the trail leading to the water. A prickle of unease tickled the back of her neck. If she went further, she'd be out of viewing distance from the house.

Pepper glanced back, as some of her common sense deserted her.

Part of her was dying to be alone with Ñico, and part of her was scared to death to be alone with him. She crossed her arms. Her body stiffened, along with her resolve. "We have privacy now. So talk!"

"Oh?" Moonlight highlighted straight white teeth when Ñico flashed a warm smile. "I'll throw your question back at you. What is your problem, *querida*? What are you afraid of?" His all-knowing grin grew, one that said he knew exactly what she was afraid of.

"What game do you play, Ñico?"

He sobered, eyeing her intently. "Do you see marriage and commitment as a game?"

"No. Of course not." Her jaw clenched and she straightened her back, one vertebra at a time.

"You made a promise. One I'm holding you to."

"What about you? Do you intend to remain faithful if we marry?"

Ñico exhaled on one long sigh. "I've never felt about another as I feel about you." He reached out and undid the clip from her hair, releasing its heavy fullness as it fell in a dark blanket around her bare arms and shoulders. His hand lifted, touching and fingering a thick strand, seeming to luxuriate in its feel.

"You are so beautiful." He secured a handful and took it to his lips, grazing back and forth. "I love your hair. I could get lost in its texture and richness forever."

Pepper closed her eyes, fighting the impulse to give in to the need elicited by his hot, vibrant voice, filled with so much more than mere words. She pushed it away, strengthening her determination to remain aloof. She opened her eyes and pierced him with a stare, daring him to speak the truth. "That doesn't answer my question."

"I want you. I've never wanted another like I do you. I admire you. I'm willing to give you my name. My worldly goods. Why is that not enough when it's more than most in our situation have?"

A sad smile formed. He sounded so like Felipe, spouting their native island's stubborn male mantra. "Why can't you see my side of the issue?"

"Your side?"

"What about love? Don't you want to love your wife?"

"You're a dreamer." Ñico chuckled softly, the sound wafting past her ears like the kiss of death, killing all hopes, stabbing the knife deeper into her heart. "Love doesn't exist for people like us."

She blocked out the pain and met his gaze, holding the misery his statement produced inside. "You're so sure?"

His eyebrow lifted. "Are you saying you love me?"

How could she admit what she felt? Not when he scoffed at the emotion and would use it to bind her to him. Pepper shook her head. "I don't know what I'm saying." Her voice trailed off when he dropped his handful of hair and placed both hands on her shoulders, pulling her closer.

"Look at our role models. The best we can hope for is what we already have. Why ruin it with unattainable expectations. We do well together, *querida*. Especially in the bedroom." His head descended. "I have only to do this and you melt."

Soft lips touched hers and drew a soft moan. She shouldn't want his kiss, but she couldn't think of anything she'd rather have at the moment. Of their own volition, her hands enveloped his neck, closing their separating gap. Unrestrained desire erupted, negating any other mental opposition. She no longer cared that she'd been like sculpting putty in his hand during dinner, that he'd stroked and molded her passion with little touches and innuendos, smoldering glances, and secret smiles. It didn't matter that he'd eventually break her heart; she no longer could deny her need. Not when his mouth and tongue were yanking it out of her, with kiss after kiss after kiss after kiss. Mercy, did he know how to kiss.

Ñico broke away. Nipped the tip of her nose. Then he grabbed her hand as he unlatched the gate, and pulled her with him.

All resistance had melted as he'd predicted, compliments of one scorching moment in Ñico's arms. Pepper followed, with absolute certainty this was not in her best interest. Despite wearing an elegant strapless gown and heels not conducive to hiking along a bluff, she hurried to keep up. More than anything, she had to finish what his mouth had begun.

Once down the hilly trail, they strolled toward the water's edge.

Halfway there, Ñico shrugged out of his dark jacket and began loosening his tie.

Pepper laughed. "What are you doing?"

"Isn't it obvious? I'm undressing."

"Someone will see," she hissed in whispers. She cast a worried glance over her shoulder to check out the house, barely visible in the dark night. What if someone was out on the deck and noticed?

"No one will bother us. Despite the moonlight, we're shrouded in darkness." He took off his shoes and socks before dropping his pants and stepping out of them. "It's the perfect cover for lovemaking."

"Ñico!" She was shocked, but too enraptured to do much more than watch.

He stopped in the process of stripping off his underwear, a boxer/briefs combination encasing his butt in a tight sheath, and looked up, catching her focus. Eyes locked on hers. He pushed the stretchy material down releasing his full erection, the entire time gripping her attention. Kicking out of the bit of fabric, he tossed it aside before his hand went to his erection, stroking, his heated gaze yelling, *See what you do to me?* Then, sliding fingers to the front of his shirt, he slowly undid one button at a time.

Pepper choked on the breath she'd been holding, unable to look away. Unable to inhale. His teasing actions did strange things to her insides. Though her experience with such flaunting exhibitionism was limited, she decided she loved watching him strip. He set his shirt on the sand with his suit and straightened to his full six feet two inches of height, totally naked. Noting the proud conquistador before her, his huge erection pulling her focus, she sucked in a ragged breath, then swallowed, hard. The thumping of her heartbeat became noticeable as her pulse increased. Dear Lord, he was beautiful.

"Well, *querida*?" Ñico quirked an eyebrow. "Are you going to stand there gawking, or are you going to join me?"

Did she dare?

Vacillating, her tongue made a sweep of her lips. She spared one more glance over her shoulder, noting no movement in the darkness.

He was probably right about being alone and hidden in the shadowy night.

Giggling, Pepper kicked off first one shoe and then the other. It was easy to slip out of her fully lined gown, undoing the zipper with a quick yank. She stepped out of lacy, body-hugging underwear, having long ago given up pantyhose because of the humidity. In seconds, she bent to place her dress neatly in the sand and was caught from behind.

Her shriek filled the air as he easily lifted her, carrying her toward the water. His erection poked her bottom, and while he walked, she couldn't quite quell the excitement zinging through her body such contact caused. Every nerve she possessed stood at full alert.

Waiting.

Oh, how she wanted him inside her. "I'm heavy!" she cried out with a loud giggle.

"Shush." Ñico chuckled near her ear, the rich sound conveying more sensation heading straight to her middle. "You'll draw attention with your screams. Your father's already upset with me for making love with you." He nibbled her lobe, his tongue stroking. A burst of white-hot pleasure spread tingles of excitement everywhere. "I'm pretty sure if we're caught naked together, you will no longer have a choice. He'll be forcing our marriage with a shotgun."

"Don't drop me," she said, laughing, gripping his neck in an effort to hold on. At this point, her experience would be worth the consequence he mentioned. Pepper was having too much fun to give her father a second thought now. Never had she considered herself as someone who'd be bold enough to make love like this, out in the open with the night as the only cover.

"What? You think I'm not strong enough to carry you? That I might let you go?" Nico loosened his hold and she slipped a bit, causing her to shriek again. He laughed, hugging her and planting a kiss on her neck. "You're too damned sexy. I'd never drop you. Not now, when I have you right where I want you."

Warm water lapped against her feet once he waded deep enough, the effect of the temperature difference negligible to the night air. He kept going until they were deeper. Waves washed over them. Then she felt him sinking into the warm water. He reinforced his hold, at the same time shifting, bringing her closer before his mouth found hers.

Moonlight glistened on the ocean, presenting a seductive backdrop. His hands caressed, leaving no part of her body untouched. The sound of the waves hitting the shore was background music, all of it inciting her senses in a rush of emotion. She'd never given much thought to how arousing kissing a man while surrounded with an ocean of water could be, but she was totally aroused. Totally in tune to Nico and his body, with what his touch was doing to her. In moments, all coherent thought fled as his fullness filled her, moving in that age-old rhythm, seducing her further, drawing a more acute awareness of the man stroking her insides with his thickness than she ever thought possible. As if he'd given a silent command, Pepper's legs circled his waist and she held on tighter for the wet, wild, driving ride. She flowed with the waves, pleasure growing and pulsating while he thrust. She could stay here forever wrapped around him in blissful ecstasy. Wave after wave of sensation rippled over her in conjunction with the Caribbean's swells, until her orgasm burst forth in one encompassing splash of pleasure. Seconds later, Nico followed.

I love you, her mind shouted, after the sensations of her release slowly faded, leaving only contentment behind. But she didn't dare vocalize the words. If Nico knew of her feelings, she had no doubt he'd use the knowledge to manipulate her into marriage. In a heartbeat, contentment fled as the reality of her situation struck. Pepper had no willpower where he was concerned, not when he kissed her like he had and then filled her with his essence. She'd loved this man since she was a child and as an adult, the feelings intensified a million times over, especially when in the throes of passion. Her body recognized and reacted to her soul mate's call.

Damn if she wasn't her mother's daughter after all.

Tears trickled down the side of her face. She brushed them away, not wanting him to know how the agony of loving him tore at her. How would she hold on to herself? Not be sucked into the vortex of his vital personality? It would be much easier to marry him if she didn't love him.

"*Querida?*"

His soft question drew her gaze. In the moonlight, she glimpsed the concern reflected in his eyes.

"Are you crying?" Ñico's hand touched her face. "I didn't hurt you, did I?"

Too choked up to speak, she shook her head, blinking back more tears.

"I'm sorry." He kissed her cheek and hugged her to him. "But I lose control, moving with you like that." He grinned, then chuckled, squeezing her tighter. "The earth moves when we make love, *querida*. Do you not feel it?"

Pepper nodded.

"Do you not see how well we do together? We're made for each other. Surely you recognize this?"

She shivered, the coolness of the breeze suddenly becoming noticeable. But it wasn't just the wind causing goose bumps. His observations sent a sliver of regret up her spine. They *were* made for each other. Soul mates. Only she'd never own his soul. Not like he owned hers.

"You're cold. We should go inside." He stood, clutching her tightly, with her limbs still surrounding him. Slowly, his hold loosened and her legs relaxed. She slid the length of his lower body, breaking their contact, and stood.

Ñico held out his hand, smiling warmly. "Come, the evening isn't over. We still have to talk."

Hand in hand, she silently followed her naked, proud

conquistador out of the water. He led her toward the discarded items in the sand.

Both were dripping wet with no towel to soak up the excess salt water and sand clung to their feet.

"We'll ruin our clothes if we put them on now," she murmured, suddenly feeling self-conscious.

"They can be dry-cleaned."

"But who will stop the servants from talking when they notice why they need to be dry-cleaned?" She could just imagine their gossip, which was a good as putting an ad in the newspaper. Her parents would learn of their late-night swim within minutes and draw their own conclusions. Then she'd find herself with no choice at all, just as Ñico had teased about earlier. "No sense waving a red flag in front of my father."

"Hmmm. Good point." He stroked his chin, glancing back at the house. "You distracted me and I wasn't thinking clearly."

Pepper groaned inwardly, rolling her eyes. She certainly hadn't been using her brain. Somehow rational thought had a way of disappearing when Ñico kissed her. She'd have to be more careful in the future.

"Let's sneak into your room to shower." In a quick move, he tugged at her arm, throwing her off balance. Then, still holding her with a firm grip, he swooped lower, kissing her thoroughly, before his lips roamed along her jaw and across her neck. "Then we can talk," he whispered, spending long seconds nibbling on her ear.

Mercy, she should be stronger. Yet thoughts of them showering together filled her mind, weakening her determination. Her suite of rooms had a door leading outside she'd kept unlocked, but if caught sneaking in naked, they'd face the same outcome. A forced marriage.

Despite the threat, she wasn't ready to end her time with Ñico. Not just yet. So when he let her go and seized her hand, pulling her behind him as he bent to grab their clothes, she meekly took her gown and sandals and hiked up the trail without a word.

His promised talk had nothing to do with her motives. It was, in fact, the last thing on her mind.

While they walked, Pepper's heart pounded in anticipation, in excitement. She couldn't control the exhilaration racing through her veins. Nearing the side of the house where her darkened rooms were located, a giggle burst forth at the absurdity of sneaking Ñico into her domain, both naked as the marble sculptures of Greek gods that guarded the front door.

If her roommates saw her now, they wouldn't recognize her. She didn't recognize herself. She'd become a wanton. A glutton for physical pleasure. A thrill-seeker. Everything about her life since she'd met Ñico was thrilling.

Once inside, Ñico's expression said it all. As if on cue, they both dropped their clothes, then fell into each other's arms in a flurry of touching and kissing.

Mouths and hands explored.

"You're cold," he murmured, breaking contact and kissing her forehead when she shivered. She smiled, remaining speechless, knowing full well her shivers weren't so much from the cold, but from what his nearness generated. No! She wasn't a bit cold, not when the heat of his body warmed her.

"Come." Ñico caught her hand, leading her toward the bathroom. "A shower will warm you."

A shower would work, she thought dreamily, following him.

After long minutes in the steaming heat with hot water cascading, they stroked each other—lathers of soap sliding up and down arms, torsos, and bottoms, grazing each other. Teasing with touches. Eventually, mouths followed hands. Soon, both were too engrossed in lovemaking to bother with washing any lingering sand and salt off their skin. This coupling was slow. Unhurried. Pepper felt like she was in an erotic dream, her every movement drawn out as Ñico leisurely touched and kissed her. And she leisurely touched and kissed him. He entered her, pushing her back against the cool marble. He thrust, impaling her with his fullness and painstakingly pulled out, little by little, extracting her low moans, before thrusting again and repeating the process. Over and over and over and over. When her world shattered in an explosion of intense pleasure, for one long moment she surely thought she'd die from loving him.

Cold water startled both out of their after-lovemaking lethargy, a reminder they still stood in the shower. Laughing, Ñico broke their connection and shut off the faucet. He grabbed a towel and wrapped her in its luxurious thickness. He quickly dried off, then bent to pick Pepper up, carrying her to the bed. The single bed seemed too small for both of them with his big frame, but they fit when she lay on her side with him spooning. Barely. For how long they remained connected, her backside nestled against his groin, she didn't know. All she knew was that she felt too sated and comfortable to move.

When the air conditioner kicked on and cool air hit them, she realized her head was still soaking wet. She lifted up.

Ñico's arms tightened. "Where are you going?" He nuzzled, kissing her neck.

"My hair's still wet." She pulled away and disengaged from his arms and legs. "I need to dry it, or it'll stay wet all night."

Once up, she dragged a dryer out of her suitcase, plugged it in, and bent from the waist. After thirty seconds of drying, she felt his hands on her shoulders.

"Here, let me do that." Ñico then situated her on the floor, with her back to him in between his knees while he sat on the bed. Aiming the dryer, he drew his fingers through her hair, blowing hot air at the same time.

Content to let him work, she sighed, enjoying the feel of his hand sifting through her long strands, lifting and separating the dark masses while he dried. He kept the dryer moving, systematically working the device around her head. The hot air felt good, like a blanket of warmth in the air-conditioned coolness.

"I love your hair."

Pepper grunted in acknowledgement. She loved her hair too, except for those times when the length and thickness seemed too much trouble.

"It takes forever to dry, which is why I rarely wash it at night." It was much easier just to wash it and let it go in the morning, securing the damp length with a scrunchie to dry naturally. "It's too long."

"It's exquisite." Ñico held up a handful, still blowing, then released it to fall around her shoulders. "Such a rich color and so thick. I could get lost in this hair."

She grinned and said off-handedly, "I'm thinking of cutting it." She placed her chin on her knee and sighed. "Maybe having it styled."

"No!" He flicked the switch, letting the hair dryer drop, then wound strands around his fingers and tugged her to face him. "I prefer it long," he murmured before his mouth lowered. He nipped and kissed playfully. "Which means you can't cut it."

"What? Let me get this straight." She turned around to see his expression, eyeing him warily. "You want my hair long. So I can't cut it?"

"Why would you?" Ñico planted a kiss on her forehead, offering a lop-sided grin. "It's beautiful, just the way it is."

"Long hair isn't in vogue unless you're a kid." Pepper waved his good-natured teasing away with the back of her hand. Her chin settled on her knee again. "I should've styled it years ago."

"I treasure your hair. Such tresses shouldn't be touched with scissors, *querida*."

A steely resolve not present a moment ago slid into his voice. After spending a few days getting to know Ñico, Pepper recognized the subtle affectation. "It's my hair, and my decision," she said in an effort to assert her position. The man could be a bit controlling. "And I'm quite tired of having a furnace on my head."

"And as your future husband, I'm telling you not to cut it."

She stiffened, raising her head and turning so she could once again meet his gaze. Her eyebrows rose. "Oh?" Despite his earlier lighthearted manner, the teasing glint had vanished. Ñico's eyes now reflected total seriousness. "You're *telling* me not to cut it?" *No one* would *tell* her what she could and could not do. Not now. Not ever.

His hands gripped her face, fingers gently stroking. "No, *querida*!" He shook his head, his expression still intent. "I'm asking you. I love your hair. Please don't cut it."

Eyeing him thoughtfully, Pepper chewed on the inside of her cheek, neither agreeing nor disagreeing.

"Your hair is too beautiful to cut." As if the subject was closed, he signaled with his hand, finger circling. "Turn around and I'll finish. Then we can talk."

Silently, she did as he asked. He resumed drying.

He shut off the power and set the dryer aside. "We need to discuss the conversation you overheard this afternoon."

She shrugged. "There's nothing to discuss."

"I'd like to explain why I spoke so bluntly." With a thumb and forefinger, Ñico tilted her chin, forcing her to look into his eyes. "Your father can be a bit abrasive and confrontational." He snorted. "Much like my own."

Pepper smiled. "Tell me something I don't know."

Nodding, Ñico's grin expanded. "I'm glad you comprehend how it is." Then his smile died. "I didn't lie to Miguel when I told him how I felt about a possible pregnancy. Only not for the reasons I stated. I admire your independence. I cherish your feistiness and look forward to our skirmishes. I certainly don't want to change you, but understand this. I would love nothing better than to learn you carry my babe. And if a pregnancy results from our lovemaking, we will marry."

Such confidence he exuded in his boastful statements. Pepper wasn't worried about pregnancy. Her "friend" was due any day now, so she felt safe enough. For the moment.

"And," he continued. "I can think of no better woman to bear my seed. I want you to have my child, *querida.*" Ñico brushed her hair off her shoulder and kissed the skin below her neck. "I want a dozen children with you."

"I doubt I'm pregnant, but if I was, what about love?" She ignored the delicious sensations his softly circling fingers created, leaning away from the contact. "Don't you think children deserve parents who love each other?" Though she already knew his views, she couldn't stop the questions from popping out.

He sighed, shaking his head. "I've never met anyone as stubborn as you."

"I could say the same." Why couldn't he abandon his antiquated ideas? If only he was capable of returning her love.

"Do you deny what we have together? This yearning between us grows. You do understand if we continue, you'll eventually end up pregnant?" He wrapped a hand around her hair and lifted her head. "Tell me you don't feel it!"

Why can't it include love, she wanted to shout. Instead, she rose in compliance with the unspoken request spilling from his expression. His head lowered in slow motion. Mouths grazed, connecting with the barest touch. Back and forth. At the same time both descended onto the bed. He positioned her underneath, maintaining his almost kisses. Then his tongue traced her lips. He groaned, melding his mouth to hers, as their passion ignited like a lit match hitting tinder.

Breathing heavily, Ñico lifted his head. "Can you stop this?"

"No," she whispered, closing her eyes, working to remain calm, yet hating the fact that he could draw out her yearning so effortlessly. Pepper opened her eyes and met his heated gaze. "I meant what I said. I'll not be pushed into marriage. Pregnant or not." She dared not confide her true feelings, nor did she let them seep into her expression. She certainly couldn't admit the thought of having his child sounded too appealing. She would love to have his baby. At least she'd have something of him. Right now, she simply wanted more than the results of great sex. "Maybe you should use protection."

Ñico chuckled. "Maybe I should. But we can discuss this later." He planted a few kisses on her face, his mouth traveling the distance to her ear. "It's getting late. I need to go." He extricated himself from her limbs, then rose and began dressing. "I'll be back at eight in the morning to pick you up, so be ready."

"Why?" Pepper stretched, stifling a yawn. Watching him covering his body with clothes wasn't the same titillating experience as watching him strip.

"I want to show you some of the projects I'm working on around the island." He fastened the last button on his shirt before tucking it into dark trousers. "You've been gone awhile. There are many changes I'm sure you'll like." He draped his tie around his neck, letting it hang loose, then sat and put on shoes and socks. "I'll give you a tour. We'll spend the day together, and you can see what I do."

"Okay. I'll be ready at eight."

"*Bien.*" Ñico leaned closer and wrapped his hands in her hair. He tugged, their lips connecting in a last heated kiss. "I hate leaving you," he whispered, nipping at her mouth.

"Hmmm." She smiled, enjoying his lingering lips. "It is too bad you have to go."

"If we were married, I could stay all night. I'd never have to leave."

She remained silent, not rising to his baiting.

After eyeing her for long seconds, Ñico stood. Chuckling, he said, "*Hasta la vista, querida.*" Then he bent to add a chaste kiss on her forehead. "I'll see you in the morning."

Seconds later the door closed behind his departing form. As she viewed the vacant space he'd just occupied, a sudden wave of loneliness engulfed her. He'd been gone less than a minute, yet his absence left a gaping hole in her heart. A tear broke free after she spied his imprint in the pillow. She didn't want to feel the emptiness, but she did. Too much.

Pepper switched off the bedside lamp. She lay in the darkness, eyes focused on the ceiling, wishing he didn't possess her soul. Why did it have to be Antonio Fernández who made her feel this way? How would she ever survive loving him?

Chapter 11

"I'll get it." Pepper jumped up from the breakfast table at the sound of the doorbell. "That's Ñico."

"Oh?" Her mother's eyebrows rose. "He's calling fairly early this morning."

"We're spending the day together. He's going to show me some of his projects on the island."

"How nice, Peppita. As his future wife, you should take an interest in his work." Her father patted Elena's hand and smiled.

Pepper hurried out of the dining room toward the front door, ignoring the silent message passing between her parents. Nothing, not her father's comment nor their speculative glances, would ruin her joy at seeing Ñico today. She was determined to learn more about him. Maybe, just maybe, if they spent enough time with each other and she became enmeshed in his life on the island, he'd fall in love with her, as she had with him.

She opened the door and grinned, eyeing the sexy hunk in front of her. "Right on time."

"*Querida*." Ñico offered her a small bouquet of wildflowers. "These reminded me of you. Colorful and wild. You look beautiful as always."

"Thank you." Pepper took the flowers and moved aside so he could enter. He was handsome in daylight, wearing casual slacks and a polo shirt. As usual the expensive clothes fit him as if they were made for his lean, muscular build, adding to the power he exuded. The lopsided grin he sported did strange things to her insides. Though there was nothing boyish about the man who stood so proudly before her, how had she not recognized him when his smiling countenance was so similar to the boy in her memories?

She turned to put the bouquet in water, but Ñico's hand on

her arm stopped her. She glanced back with the question in her eyes, even as it felt as though the temperature in the room went up ten degrees.

"I've waited much too long to do this," he murmured, hauling her into his arms and lowering his head.

The instant their lips connected, all thoughts of flowers emptied from Pepper's mind. Still clutching the bouquet, her hands snuck around his neck. For long seconds, she did nothing but let the surge of pleasure his mouth and the soft touch of his stroking fingers elicited spread throughout her system. Oh, did Ñico know how to kiss. Would she ever get enough of this drugging, mindless bliss?

When someone cleared his throat behind them, she guiltily broke free.

Her father stood a mere ten feet away, and Pepper's arms fell to her sides. Her gaze lowered as her face flamed. It was one thing to mention sex in front of a parent, but to be caught in the act of something so intimate was another, and entirely disconcerting.

"Ñico." Miguel acknowledged him with a slight nod. "I'm glad to see you two are getting on so well."

Of course he'd say that, Pepper thought, smoothing her slacks. Her father was almost gloating.

Ñico dropped one arm, but kept the other firmly around her in a possessive embrace as he planted a chaste kiss on her forehead. Then, as cool as a frosted drink on a hot day, he shook her father's outstretched hand, not the least bit frazzled.

"Miguel." Ñico grinned. "You should give a person more warning."

Pepper chewed on the inside of her cheek wishing she could remain as unfazed.

"Obviously." Miguel grunted. "But if I did, I wouldn't see much, now would I?" He let go of Ñico's hand and added, "Pepper said you're giving her a tour of the island. Make sure you take her by the school your company designed."

Pepper's eyebrows lifted and her gaze flew to Ñico's. "School?"

"You'll see," was all he said, leading her out the door, seeming in a rush to leave all of a sudden.

"Wait." She pulled out of his grasp. "I have to put my flowers in water or they'll die."

"Hurry. I'm anxious to get started."

She almost ran, unwilling to leave her father and Ñico alone any longer than necessary. Separately, they were barely manageable. Who knew what the two would think up if she gave them a chance to talk?

Once her flowers were dealt with, she sidled up behind them and caught her father saying, "Make sure you do."

Ñico looked up and though he smiled, she could tell by the stiff line of his back he was annoyed. Plus, his smile didn't quite reach his eyes.

"Good! You're finally ready." He nodded to her father. "If you'll excuse us? Pepper and I have a busy day ahead."

Miguel waved them off.

Without a word, Ñico led her to an open jeep with a roll bar. When both were seated and he started the engine, she asked, "So, what was that all about?"

"What?" He stopped with his hand on the gearshift, eyeing her with a blank expression.

"Nice try." Pepper crossed her arms. "I recognize male posturing when I see it. What were you and my father discussing before I interrupted? I was gone less than a minute."

"It was nothing I couldn't handle." Another smile took over his face, only this one encompassed his eyes.

"Ah. That's right. You're good at handling, aren't you?" Mercy, he had such a sexy smile.

"It *is* one of my many talents." His gaze zeroed in on her mouth, which together with his steamy voice sent tiny zings of pleasure straight to her tummy, giving her an idea of exactly what talents he meant. There was something delicious in the way his eyes lingered, as if he'd been in the desert too long without water, and her lips were a spring runoff after a snowy winter.

"Your point?"

Ñico's voice drew her out of her sensual musings. He now watched her intently. The heat emanating from those dark coffee eyes, a torched fire blazing, still spoke too blatantly. She had no doubt he read her thoughts as easily as the morning paper.

117

She shook her head to clear her mind and cast off the effects of his seductive powers. The man already wielded too much influence over her. No sense giving him more ammunition.

"No point," she finally said, trying not to sound like a lovesick fool.

He chuckled, as the warmth reflected in his eyes morphed into amusement. Of course, her attempts to remain unaffected hadn't fooled him.

She inhaled a steadying breath. "Just letting you know I'm aware of your nonverbal cues. My father said something to annoy you. I'd like an explanation."

Ñico didn't reply. His attention turned to shifting gears. He backed out of the space and seconds later they were driving on Isla del Diablo's main road.

"Humph." Pepper kept her arms crossed and peered out the window. She should have expected his reaction. He was so like her father and Felipe, thinking they controlled everything just because they were men. Angrily, she tapped her foot and focused on the passing scenery to occupy her thoughts. When they'd driven miles from the house, her curiosity got the better of her.

"Well?" she finally asked.

"Well what?"

"Aren't you going to tell me?"

"No."

"You were discussing me, weren't you?"

"Maybe. But I refuse to let minor annoyances disturb our time together, *querida*."

"Okay," she murmured, noting the determined set of his jaw. That, together with his firm tone meant the subject was closed. But neither did much to stop her mind from churning.

Ñico didn't seem the type to let anyone coerce him, but what if both fathers were pressuring him at the same time? She knew from experience how persuasive Miguel Delgado was. And Paulo Fernández was cut from the same bolt of fabric; their willfulness weaved with the same tenacious threads of grit that made them wealthy business leaders of Isla del Diablo. Of course, Ñico was one of them, or wanted to be. He'd cave to their machinations, as well as learn how to utilize them.

"Your expression is too grave." He gripped her knee and squeezed. "Care to share what you're thinking?"

Pepper glanced at him. "No." If he didn't want to share his thoughts, she certainly wasn't going to elaborate on hers. She shook her head, holding back a smile, but it tugged free. She had a hard time not smiling around Ñico.

By now, they'd driven to the other side of the island. Like most islands dotting the Caribbean, Isla del Diablo wasn't huge. Getting around the one hundred and twenty square miles of land surrounding an inactive volcano wasn't too daunting. Cars were expensive to import, so most islanders relied on scooters and bikes, along with public transportation.

When he slowed in front of a building that hadn't been standing four years earlier, her eyebrows rose. "This is new. In fact, I've noticed a lot of other changes."

During the twelve-mile drive, she'd noted many new houses or gardens had replaced vacant lots, along with a few buildings. Due to the founding fathers' belief in education and a pervading idealism and social philosophy, her island had never been poverty-stricken, unlike some of its neighbors. The men who controlled the economic livelihood of the island, including Pepper's and Ñico's fathers, kept the standard of living high, holding the islanders up to certain expectations. Native families, their simple needs consisting of basics like food, clothing, and housing, made their own way and lived within their means.

"There are many changes. I've been busy trying to create more," Ñico said, in reply to her comment.

He pulled into a space and shut off the ignition before setting the brake. Then he climbed out and ran around to her side, taking her arm to assist her out of the jeep.

He placed an arm around her shoulders and steered her toward the entrance, adding as they walked, "I think someone with your love of the island will find the changes good. Especially this one." At the door, Pepper waited until he opened it. "It's a new venture for Fernández Industries."

"New venture?" She glanced around once inside. "Looks like a school."

"It is. A high school. Not only do students learn math,

language arts, and reading, we extended the curriculum to include anything else a student might need to develop better skills to find employment or create a business on Isla del Diablo. Exceptional students can get scholarships and add a year or two to continue and move into a curriculum that includes management."

"Good afternoon, *Señor* Fernández." Pepper wasn't surprised to hear the woman's perfect English. Most islanders spoke English, the official language since Pepper had been a baby. Business leaders had determined well before then that to compete in the global world, the islanders needed a command of the global language. English was deemed a necessity and taught along with their native Spanish in the schools. One would have to search far and wide to find a person who didn't speak both languages fluently, and usually those were the older citizens who never saw a need to change.

Ñico grinned and shook the lady's outstretched hand. "May I present *Señorita* Delgado?" He turned to Pepper. "This is *Señorita* Bonita Sanchez, the principal."

"*Señorita*." She bowed. "We've been looking forward to your visit."

"Please call me Pepper." The pretty woman was barely older than she, and too much of a peer to be so formal.

"Certainly, if you'll return the favor and call me Bonita." Bonita acted friendly enough. Yet, Pepper didn't fail to notice the bit of jealousy reflected in her eyes, nor could she miss the way those eyes followed everything Ñico did. Though to give him credit, Ñico seemed oblivious to Bonita's adoration as the principal led them through a long hallway.

At first, Pepper assumed such obvious adulation was something he took for granted. But after eyeing him surreptitiously while taking in her surroundings, she discarded the idea. He clearly didn't seem to notice Bonita. Ñico's attention was riveted to her, as if gauging her reaction to what she saw. Somehow, from his stiff posture and intense expression, she sensed her opinion mattered, in fact was his most important thought. Her idea solidified after continuing the tour.

Bonita stopped at the door of a classroom and knocked.

Another young woman opened the door and smiled.

"*Señora* Mendoza," Bonita said. "You remember *Señor* Fernandez. This is *Señorita* Delgado."

"Welcome," *Señora* Mendoza said, opening the door wider.

Pepper ignored the way the gorgeous woman's gaze also lingered a bit too long on Nico. Being married didn't stop the teacher from drooling. Though he only spared the *señora* a brief nod now, would Nico find her someone he might stray with after he tired of Pepper? If only he wasn't so handsome and the women on the island weren't competition.

Señora Mendoza closed the door once they stepped into her classroom. She pivoted and clapped twice, drawing Pepper out of her depressing thoughts. "Class, *Señor* Fernández has come to visit. Who wants to explain what we are working on?"

Immediately hands shot up, the eagerness to display their knowledge written across twenty faces.

Pepper listened to the exchange between teacher and students with interest until the demonstration ended and they continued the tour, visiting similar classes. Everywhere she looked, she saw teenage children diligently working to learn. Though the teachers had complete control of their classrooms, the atmosphere was friendly and non-threatening, full of laughter and warmth. The perfect place for academic excellence in progress.

"Well, what do you think?" Nico asked, after they'd inspected half a dozen classrooms.

"Impressive." Pepper bit her lip in an attempt to hold on to her giggle. He reminded her of a brilliant kid wanting a pat on the head for bringing home a perfect report card. Even evident success from an overachiever still needed acknowledgement. "This is wonderful."

"*Señor* F! *Señor* F," a kid shouted after stepping inside a big gym, which Bonita indicated would conclude their tour.

A second later a basketball zoomed straight for them. Nico easily caught the ball, then leaned into a practiced dribbling move. In seconds, other kids surrounded him, breaking into two teams. They'd obviously played together before.

Pepper stood off to the side, full of curiosity, amazed to see another facet of the same man who'd spent much energy the evening before ensuring her every pleasure now actively running down the court with a bunch of teenagers.

The game continued in earnest until Ñico stopped, holding on to the ball. Laughing, he secured it between his arm and body, making a *T* with his hands. "Time out. You guys are killing me. I'm not dressed for an all-out massacre." He kicked up his foot, presenting deck shoes under his slacks. "I don't even have the right shoes."

"Oh, man. Those shoes work."

"How about a replay later?" He tossed the ball to the kid.

"Cool! You're on, old man."

Ñico chuckled and walked toward Pepper.

She grinned. "You didn't tell me you could play basketball."

"What?" He winked. "My playing skills aren't limited to the bedroom, *querida*."

"Hush, Ñico." Her face heated up. She cleared her throat and smoothed her hair, brushing her ponytail aside. But the kids were too busy yelling and laughing to take notice.

"Is she your fiancée? Introduce us."

Ñico introduced her to teenagers he knew well enough to be on a first-name basis.

When the bell rang, the impromptu party broke up. The gym quickly emptied of everyone but Ñico and Pepper. Even Bonita had left them.

When she met his gaze, Ñico's eyebrows rose. "Are you ready to continue?"

Pepper nodded, then followed him to the jeep. He opened her door.

"I'm impressed. Isla del Diablo needed such a school." When she'd left four years ago, some of the hotels were recruiting workers from Puerto Rico and elsewhere rather than employ island natives. Those owners felt the locals too unsophisticated to work in five-star resorts.

"This is only the beginning. You've seen very little so far."

Before climbing inside, she gave one last glance at the school he'd funded and built. Ñico's efforts to circumvent future problems by teaching and training workers on utilizing the island's natural resources was an effective means to keep the islanders gainfully employed.

"I didn't realize you had such a soft spot for kids." Pepper clicked her seat belt into place.

"I love kids." He grinned. "Did you think I jested when I mentioned wanting a dozen?"

She sighed. Of course, he was serious. She looked out the window again, ignoring the way the statement filled her with pleasure. He'd make a wonderful father, despite not making a wonderful husband.

For the rest of the morning he showed off his investments—an office building, a couple of shopping centers, and several restaurants—all of which needed the skilled employees his school provided.

They ate a delicious lunch in one of those restaurants on the water. Then he gave her a quick tour of the resort hotel he owned, including a dolphin refuge connected with the hotel and utilized as an aquarium. The beauty of this setup was the natural habitat. Thousands of fish and mammals swam in a sheltered cove, free to come and go at will, giving the tourists a more realistic look at life underwater through glass.

After spending these hours with Ñico, she viewed him differently. He wasn't just a playboy seeking the next conquest or thrill. In fact, she saw nothing of that Ñico in the man beside her.

"How did you manage to do all this in such a short time?" she asked, when he pulled into the parking lot of one of the taller structures on the island. Nothing of what she'd toured had existed four years earlier.

FERNÁNDEZ INDUSTRIES. The bigger-than-life sign denoting a new state-of-the-art building said it all.

"I told you I was trying to impress my *padré*." He shrugged. "I now am glad I did, because I find I like impressing you." He turned off the jeep's ignition and faced her. "Shall we move on to the finale?"

She nodded, eyeing his pleased expression.

Oh yes! Ñico Fernández was more than a mere businessman. He had vision. He loved Isla del Diablo as much as she did. This came out in every investment he'd detailed, and he hadn't exaggerated. The amount of growth stunned her. The island bustled with activity, productivity, and economic development, no doubt the result of Ñico's efforts. He *had* achieved a great deal in such a short time. His father should be proud. Very few men could attain as much in a lifetime, much less in four years.

"*Señor* Fernández." A man nodded on his way out, holding the door open for them. "How nice to see you."

Several people said much the same thing as they walked toward the bank of elevators.

Ñico nodded and addressed each one by name, offering a friendly smile while he introduced her as his fiancée.

Pepper didn't correct him, unconcerned with what excuse he'd use when she returned to Florida. That was his problem, not hers. He seemed to be well-liked. The easygoing way those who greeted him emphasized how comfortable they felt in his company. But she also noted the way their voices held respect and genuine affection. Definitely showing another facet to the man, and not the reaction she expected toward someone as controlling as she knew Ñico to be.

"Why did you introduce me as your fiancée?" she asked, once the steel doors closed.

"Why not? It's how I view you. You're mine. I want to make sure everyone knows it."

She swallowed her irritation the comment evoked. "I belong to no one."

"Maybe I should rephrase." Ñico chuckled. "I want you as my wife for many reasons, but I don't want to own you. I want a helpmate." He pushed the button for the top floor. "I need a strong woman by my side, someone who sees my vision for the island and can help me attain my goals."

"You want my help?"

"I know your worth, *querida*. You're a formidable woman in business as well as in the bedroom."

In a heartbeat, annoyance morphed into something more pleasant. Ignoring the sensations, she grinned and teased, "The islanders already love you and think of you as their king." Pepper's grin expanded. "Which means, if we married I could be queen of the island."

"Whether you like it or not, our roles are as leaders." He flashed the same smile that always grabbed at her insides. "You're one of them and they will love you as they do me."

Yes, but I don't want their love. I want yours, she wanted to yell. But she didn't. Instead she remained silent as the elevator rose and her mood plummeted.

When the doors opened at the top floor, Pepper followed him into a large reception area and stopped to do a three-sixty. Marble floors and walls trimmed in dark wood and accented with glass shouted success.

"My office is this way." He grabbed her hand and tugged, leading her to a huge room that was another sight for the senses. For just a moment she forgot to breathe as she glanced around. This office belonged to a man of power.

"How do you get anything done with this great view?" Pepper broke out of his grasp and strode to the wall of windows. She rubbed her arms and looked out.

Another beautiful day in paradise. Yellow, red, and green streaks of colors fanned out in the parasails and windsurfers, dotting the various shades of blue differentiating water from sky. The island had become a tourist destination, a paradise for vacationers from all parts of the globe. And they were definitely making the most of their adventures.

"Usually I'm too busy to notice." Nico came up behind her and put his hands on her shoulders. He pushed her hair out of the way and nuzzled her neck. "I can guarantee I wouldn't get much done if you stood in front of it, though."

A knock at the door had him sighing.

Pepper tried to step out of his grasp, but his hold tightened.

"I'll deal with you later." He planted another kiss on her shoulder, then released his hold and returned to his desk. "I should put in a secret entrance so they wouldn't know when I'm here. Then no one would bother me." Yet, his grin hadn't added any more weight to his words than his tone had.

He sat, saying, "Come in."

Pepper giggled and sprawled in a plush chair in front of his desk as the room filled with bodies. She had a niggling feeling they'd be here awhile. He obviously loved dealing with whatever knocked. What's more, after what she'd seen earlier, she knew he'd never ignore business.

In minutes, Ñico was pulled in twenty different directions. Phones began ringing. Pepper got caught up in his energy when he nodded for her to join him as he headed for a meeting. While walking, she noted several men and women running around, looking much like order takers on the stock exchange floor, all doing his bidding.

"This is *Señorita* Angelina Delgado," Ñico said, his no-nonsense tone introducing her to other men and one woman seated at the huge mahogany table in the conference room, another room with a killer view. How anyone got anything done was beyond her.

"I'm including her in our meeting today for her input. I'm sure any idea she has will benefit Fernández Industries." When a few grumbled, Ñico put up a hand. "She's a Delgado. And more importantly, she's run a successful business in the Florida Keys for years. We can tap her understanding of the tourist mind," he said in a firm voice discouraging further arguments. "Now then, let's get to work."

Pepper looked around at their faces. That was all they needed. A sentence or two from him and they accepted her as one of them. Everyone at the table was held in the same magnetic grip of his allure she'd experienced earlier, giving her a glimpse of another of Ñico's facets. He took charge, fielding every question with requests or more questions, delegating, holding their rapt attention. Pepper had no doubt each and every person in this room, and probably the company, would follow him anywhere. He was that charismatic.

Chapter 12

"You passed my house." Pepper's voice earned Ñico's attention.

"So I did." He slanted her a glance and nodded but he didn't reduce his speed. He was gearing up for the next phase of his carefully laid strategy.

"Where are we going now?"

"You'll see." He bit his lip to keep from laughing. Her curious expression reminded him of a child on Christmas Eve. "It's a surprise."

He meant to have her as his wife and he'd use any means possible to ensure this, he'd discovered. If he could involve Pepper in his company, letting her see the possibilities open to her, she'd have more reason to stay—just in case their physical relationship wasn't enough. Damn if he didn't deem their day together as a complete success, just as he'd hoped. Her suggestions, along with a few good observations concerning Fernández Industries' ongoing projects, won over every department head.

"A surprise?"

"Yes." This time, he couldn't contain his chuckle. Pepper's mind was definitely churning. Just as he'd noticed earlier, she was a sea sponge, soaking up everything he'd shown her. She couldn't hide her intelligence or her enthusiasm. Both shone in her eyes and came out in her every comment, her every expression. "Wait and see."

Ñico pulled into his driveway and shut off the engine. Pepper looked around before her questioning gaze caught his. "Your house, I take it?"

"Nothing escapes your notice, does it?" He jumped out at the same time she opened her door and spun around, still studying

127

her surroundings.

"I would have thought you'd own a bigger, more ostentatious house."

"Why?" For some reason, her comment bothered him. "I much prefer charm and scenery to pretentious affectations."

"Charming doesn't exactly define your office building. Impressive is a more apt description."

"That's for business. First impressions and the look of success are important when you're seeking capitalization and funding." He put the key into the lock and opened his front door, standing aside so she could go ahead of him. "My personal needs are simple."

"Simple?" She shook her head and glanced around, peeking into rooms. "I don't think so. Elegant would describe this better." Pepper walked to the wall of patio doors overlooking the ocean. "Who's your decorator? I love her taste. And you have another killer view."

Grinning, Nico looked around the room, viewing it from her vantage point. "I'm glad you appreciate my efforts."

"Your efforts?"

"I have no decorator, *querida*. I picked out the navy. The color reminds me of the ocean at night, and the lighter blues and creams remind me of the water during the day."

"It's beautiful." She ran a hand over a table he'd found at an auction. "And the furniture?" She met his gaze, her eyebrows raised.

Nico shrugged. "I prefer antiques with a history behind them, rather than the stark lines of modern furniture." He held out his hand and nodded. "Would you like a tour before dinner?"

"Dinner?"

"Yes, dinner. I'm cooking for you."

He meant to have her to himself tonight, without her parents and brother watching their every move.

Pepper walked through his house, not hiding her nosiness, peering into every nook and cranny. When she got to his bedroom, she stopped. Her eyes narrowed and she gave him a speculative look. "You're sure you didn't use a decorator?"

"I did have help," he admitted. "I asked Felipe which colors I should use on the walls to showcase the paintings."

"I love impressionist paintings. This room reminds me of Isla del Diablo. Very tropical and very Caribbean."

"Good." Nico grinned. "When we make love later, you'll feel right at home."

"Oh? You seem fairly sure we'll be intimate tonight."

"*Sí*, Angelita. I am. It's the only thing I'm sure of at the moment."

"Humph." She crossed her arms, sticking out her chin. "Don't count on it. I'm only here because I'm curious about you."

"Of course you are." His grin stretched. She never ceased to amuse him. They were definitely well suited. The more he was with her, the more he meant to have her as his wife. She'd eventually give up this ridiculous notion of fidelity. She was a Delgado, after all. She had to be well aware of the absurdity of her request.

He held out his hand. "Come and keep me company while I wait on you."

"I like the sound of that," Pepper said, giggling and gripping his fingers as he led her into his kitchen.

After sharing a wonderful moonlit dinner on his patio, with the noise of the waves hitting the shores blending in with the background music, a slow number began.

Nico pushed away from the table and stood. "This is our dance, *querida*."

Pepper laughed. "First you ply me with wine and delicious food, then you sweep me off my feet with dancing by moonlight?" She sighed and stepped into his arms. "How romantic."

He smiled. His grip tightened as she placed her head on his shoulder. She had to feel his desire, yet she didn't withdraw.

"Have you thought any more about marriage?" he asked.

"Umm-hmm. It's all I think about."

"Are you ready to concede? We *are* made for each other."

"Are you going to remain faithful?"

He stiffened. *Dios*, he'd never met someone so stubborn, but unwilling to spoil a wonderful evening he decided to wait for a better opportunity to broach the subject again.

That time came later that night. While making love and

before entering her, Ñico caught her gaze. "Tell me you can live without this! Marry me, *querida*. I will make you scream with pleasure every night."

She didn't answer. Not that he expected her to. And he couldn't stop from pushing his erection into her warmth, making him wonder. Who was causing whom to scream with pleasure?

Later, Ñico woke and glanced at the clock. He'd been out for an hour. Pepper still slept enfolded in his arms, but he was no longer inside her. He angled his head so he could watch her sleep, yet tightened his grip to bring her closer. Her long hair spilled along his upper chest. He reached out and fingered it, marveling at how much his wild angel attracted him. She was the most beautiful woman he'd ever seen and while gazing at her, a protective surge came over him. Why did she crave the unattainable? Why couldn't she be happy with the way things were between them? Didn't she see how good they were together, both inside and outside the bedroom?

"Come on, *querida*," he murmured, waking her. "I have to get you home."

"Okay." Languidly, Pepper reached above her, slowly stretching.

Dios, he wished he didn't have to escort her home. He wanted her in his bed and in his life. He'd have it. He'd just keep making love with her until she realized her place was with him.

~

A week later, Ñico prepared to tiptoe out of Pepper's room and make the hike to his house less than a mile down the beach. The nightly ritual had become their norm since her return. Yet tonight, he hesitated. Earlier they'd made love. And now the thought of leaving her, especially when she slept so peacefully next to him, felt like torture. Even worse, when he brought up the subject of their marriage, another recurring habit, she always brought up the issue of fidelity.

Why was she being so stubborn? When would she end this silly charade? She had to see what he saw. She belonged on the island. She was proving herself useful in his company. Her life was entangled with his. He'd made sure of it, but he was running out of time, with only days left of their original two-week deadline.

They belonged together. They were a perfect couple, especially in the bedroom. Why couldn't she be content with what they shared, which was so much more than most?

When she stirred, his focus landed on her face. Such a beautiful face.

Pepper's eyelids fluttered before opening. She met his gaze. He sucked in his breath at the desire he noted reflected in that smoldering amber gaze.

Then she smiled and he was lost. All he could do was lean toward her, his body answering the obvious questions her expression asked.

Yes! Of course, he wanted her. No! He'd never get enough of her.

Ñico's arousal grew thick as she reached for it, sliding a hand over it—back and forth. Everything moved in slow motion. He couldn't breathe. Could only feel the sensation of heat, starting at his groin and building…hot, liquid, desire…pulsating through his veins. Hands raked through the wild, untamed hair he loved, wrapping around the long strands, grasping her to him, as his lips devoured hers.

Instinct took over. He had to be inside her. Now.

Seconds after sliding into that perfect spot, she met him stroke for stroke. He furiously pumped, lost in a web of seduction.

Slow down, his mind screamed. She needs pleasure too. Somehow, he slowed his actions, but that only heightened his excitement.

When Ñico could move, he disentangled himself from her. "I should go. I hate leaving you," he whispered, nipping at her mouth.

"Hmmm." Pepper smiled, giving him more access to her neck. "I'll miss you."

"If we were married I could stay all night. I'd never have to leave," he said, repeating the same words he spoke every night. When she remained silent, he sighed. "I have an early morning meeting. Why don't you sleep in? I'll pick you up after lunch."

"Okay." She stretched.

Once dressed, he bent to kiss her forehead. "*Hasta la vista, querida*. Sleep tight." In seconds, he was heading toward the beach.

~

Pepper eyed the door Ñico had slipped out of. A sliver of regret cut through her. He always left her yearning. Tonight was no different. She hated to see the door close with finality after they'd made passionate love only minutes earlier. His scent still clung to her, and though sated, her body still tingled with need. The need to have him next to her for eternity. And earlier tonight, as he'd done too many times before, he hadn't entered her without issuing the same mandate.

"Marry me, *querida*. We're so good together."

Then he'd kissed her in that mind-numbing way of his and filled her.

She closed her eyes, still feeling the heat. If only she could block the memory.

Too many times she'd come so close to saying yes, especially in the aftermath of their lovemaking, forgetting for those glorious minutes in his arms her reasons for denying him.

Already, she felt like an addict, dependent on the pleasure he brought her.

How would she live without him…without his demanding kisses, his drugging passion, his warm endearments?

She loved him. Too much.

Pepper stared at the ceiling and sighed. Tears stung her eyes. Her resolve was dissipating, like steam rising from boiling water. Ñico's heat would eventually boil it away to nothing. She needed to do something to distance herself from the man. Something drastic. And soon. Otherwise she'd be trapped in a marriage that would only bring her heartache. The more she made love with Ñico, the worse it would be when he turned to another.

Right now, just the thought of someone replacing her sliced her heart in two.

Pepper lifted up, but her hair got caught under her elbow. She shifted, pulling her hair harder, adding to her already agitated state. She brushed it away, even as it caught again in her fingers. This time, she tossed it aside, totally annoyed. The black length weighed her down, along with her thoughts.

She should cut it. She was so tired of dealing with thick, long hair.

Then it hit her. She had her answer. She needed a new start. She needed to assert her independence. The same independence Ñico was sucking from her with his seductive ways that would eventually do her in.

This way, she could at least have some control.

She punched the pillow and pulled the sheet around her shoulders in an effort to get comfortable. Just before she drifted off to sleep, her resolve hardened.

Tomorrow she'd rectify the situation. Tomorrow she'd reclaim Pepper Delgado.

~

"Ah, Ñico! Just the person I'd like to speak with," Delgado said after opening the door, standing aside so Ñico could enter.

"Miguel," Ñico murmured, nodding. He'd been hoping he could bypass Pepper's *padré*, knowing precisely why the man waylaid him. He wanted an update on the situation.

Ñico followed the older man into his study. Delgado stalked to the bar, poured two liberal drinks, then handed him one and nodded to the chair. "Have a seat. Let's talk."

It was not a request.

Sighing, Ñico walked back to the door, searching the hallway to make sure Pepper wasn't within listening distance. He shut the door before heading for the sofa, where he sat, placing an outstretched arm along the back of the cushion, and nonchalantly sipped.

Delgado sat in the chair across from him.

Ñico silently studied the older man and waited.

"Pepper has been home for almost two weeks." Delgado crossed his legs, leaning forward. "I want a progress report."

He smiled. Of course, he did. Hadn't his own *padré* just grilled him for two hours asking much the same thing? Both men were pushing. Both wanted to know when his and Pepper's marriage would take place. "I'm still working on it."

"And how much longer are you to *work on it*?" the old man asked, his gaze narrowing. "Seems you've had plenty of nights alone, plenty of intimacy to *work on it*."

When Ñico's eyes widened in surprise, Delgado snorted. "What did you think? That no one would notice your comings and goings?" Delgado eyed him intently before waving his hand in disgust. After gulping a long drink, he met his gaze again. "I make it my business to notice. I know the exact moment you leave my daughter's room. Last night you didn't leave until two a.m. All I can say is, if I wasn't one hundred percent certain you two will be man and wife soon, you'd be a dead man." Delgado sat back, his expression grim as he pinned the younger man with his displeasure.

Others might tremble before him, but Ñico was used to overbearing old men trying to run his life through intimidation. He cleared his throat. He spent a moment taking a sip of his drink, letting the heat of the liquid warm the way to his stomach. "Your point?" he asked, quirking a brow.

"I want to know when you and Pepper will be making the trip to the altar. I expect a date."

Ñico finished his drink, swallowing the remainder in one large swig. Then he stood. "I've already given you my best answer." He set the glass on the bar and turned back to Miguel. "Your daughter is an adult, well past the age of consent. What do you think she would say if she heard your demands?"

Delgado grunted. "It's of no significance. She's my daughter. She has to know I'm not going to sit idly by while she entertains a man in her room without consequences."

Ñico laughed. "Well, despite needing all the help I can get, I'd appreciate it if you'd keep your thoughts to yourself. At least for the time being. Your *concern* is why I've had to resort to the late-night assignations. Consider it time spent overcoming our last conversation. Now if you'll excuse me, I'm late. My future wife is expecting me." He nodded and headed for the door. Gripping the knob, he turned back and added, "And I meant what I said earlier. This is between Pepper and me, so stay out of it."

Ñico closed the library door, clenching his fist in frustration. No one wanted a union with Pepper Delgado more than him. But he wanted all of her. He'd long grown tired of leaving her night after night, knowing he was so close to having it all, that if he pushed harder, she'd give in. Yet, he sensed she'd still hold part of herself back. It was that part he craved.

Why? The question stumped him. Why couldn't he just take

what she offered and be happy? Push for a win, go in for the kill, and be done with it. A woman's reticence never stopped him before. They made a good match. They definitely had more than most.

He looked up to see her floating down the stairs. When his gaze hit upon Pepper's head, he stopped and refocused on the short hairstyle.

What the hell had she done?

Her long, glorious tresses were gone.

"What did you do?" He stared, too dumbfounded to say more. She'd cut the hair he adored.

"Ñico? Do you like it?" She stopped on the middle stair and pirouetted, patting her curls. "I had my hair styled. I told you I was thinking of doing it. I should've done it years ago."

He swallowed hard as she glided toward him, smiling warmly.

She *cut* it. He couldn't believe she actually cut it when he'd told her how much he loved it. Pain nicked his heart, rendering him speechless. He had no words. Mutely, he gawked.

"Well? You didn't answer my question. What do you think?"

The style was attractive enough, but it wasn't the same. Gone were the long, thick masses he could lose himself in. Ñico shook his head. "Why are you asking what I think?" he asked, once he found his voice. "You already knew my feelings on the subject and it's obvious you disregarded them." He headed for the set of patio doors overlooking the deck. He had to get away. Her actions cut him to the core.

Chapter 13

Pepper watched him go, suddenly unsure of her actions. Had she made a huge error in judgment? She'd only been asserting her independence. She certainly never thought Ñico would be affected by something as trite as a haircut. Sure, he'd said he loved the length, but it was her hair after all and her decision, not his.

She hurried out the door after him.

Ñico." She caught up with him at the water's edge. The tide was moving out.

For long minutes, he stared off in the distance. The entire time he didn't move a muscle. She wasn't sure if he realized she stood behind him.

"Ñico?" she repeated, touching his shoulder. He stiffened, flinching away from her. She dropped her hand as if he'd burned her and waited for him to say something…anything.

Just when she was about to give up hope he'd acknowledge her, he turned and caught her gaze. The turbulence she glimpsed in his eyes had her swallowing hard. She lifted her chin. "You're making too much of this."

"Too much? I told you I love your hair and you chop it off?"

"I decided to cut it. It's my hair." Pepper's chin inched higher, daring him to refute her right.

"Yes, but you understood fully it would bother me if you cut it, especially when I asked you not to."

Commanded was more like it, but she remained mute, eyeing him stoically, neither agreeing nor disagreeing.

"Is this how you try and please me?"

His words sliced through the air, cutting into her puffed-up resolve.

Pepper took a deep breath. She couldn't back down now. Crossing her arms, she nodded. "I please myself. And if we marry, you should get used to it. You don't own me."

"I see."

Their stare-off continued, during which time, she caught something in the flicker of his eye. If Pepper didn't know better, she'd call it hurt. In the space of a heartbeat, it was gone. Unable to keep meeting his eyes, her gaze lowered. She spent a long moment studying her fingernails, before eyeing him once again, scrutinizing his face, looking for a reinforcing sentiment, but his face had become a frozen mask showing no emotion.

No. Her sigh came out in one long exhale. She was mistaken. Ñico would never love her enough to be hurt from anything she did. He'd make her scream with passion, but he'd never open his heart. "What do you see?" she asked, hiding her sorrow.

He appeared on the verge of saying something serious. Then he shook his head. "You're right. It's your hair to do with as you deem fit. I spoke out of line."

He gripped her shoulders and kissed her forehead. The old Ñico was back, yet he wasn't.

For the rest of the day, he was attentive and as charming as ever. Yet without quite determining why, Pepper intuitively felt he'd withdrawn from her.

On their way home, as he silently drove, the idea solidified. He'd shut a part of himself off, the part he'd only shared with her. And she'd come to love that veiled part. Maybe he did love her in his own way.

The thought stopped her. When he parked and climbed out of the jeep to escort her into the house, she surreptitiously studied him. Though unsettling, she couldn't deny the thought held merit. If that was true, maybe her actions had hurt him. They reached her front porch. She asked, "Ñico, are you okay?"

"I'm fine."

"You seem distracted."

"I've much to think about." His sad smile broke out. "I'm sorry. I won't be joining you for dinner. Give my regrets to your parents."

"Okay. What about later?"

"Not tonight, *querida*."

"But you've always come to my room."

"Not tonight," he repeated.

When he didn't expand, she blurted out, "Why? Is it because I cut my hair?" Pepper grabbed on to his arm when it became obvious he was just going to open the door for her and then leave. "Ñico, it'll grow back." Even she heard the desperation in her voice.

"I know." He kissed her forehead. "As I said, I've much to think about. When I first searched you out in the Florida Keys, this was not how I envisioned we would end up." After stating his words, he turned and headed toward his jeep without glancing back.

"What do you mean how we'd end up?" she yelled when he reached for the door handle. "I haven't decided yet. I still have a few days."

He pivoted, catching her gaze. "You've decided, *querida*. And the path you've decided on is not the same path I travel. You are free. I no longer wish to marry you."

"Ñico?" He didn't mean that. He couldn't. A streak of uncertainty unnerved her as her proud conquistador ignored her plea and retreated further. He started the engine and backed out, revving the motor. The irrevocability of his words didn't hit her until she faced an empty driveway after he'd driven out of sight. Was this how Scarlett felt when Rhett left?

No! Like Scarlett, Pepper wouldn't believe it. He was using it as a manipulative ploy. He'd been too adamant. Too forceful and confident to give up.

Still, she couldn't quite quell her dread at the thought that he'd truly didn't want her. The thought tugged at her, pulling at her memory until she realized why her feelings seemed so familiar. *Have I gone too far and pushed him away? Like Scarlett did Rhett?* After all, Scarlett had no idea how Rhett felt. Could she have hurt Ñico like Scarlett hurt Rhett?

Surely not, she scoffed mentally, but the doubt planted itself, settling root into her consciousness as she remembered his pragmatic words. "Scarlett blew it with Rhett." Had she blown it with Ñico?

Since Ñico didn't show for dinner, the Delgados dispensed with the formality of drinks beforehand and dined earlier. Pepper ate hurriedly, unwilling to endure more torture, and fielded her parents' questions as best she could, working to sound happy at the same time.

After dinner, she headed for the beach, hoping to see him. Maybe he'd changed his mind. She walked to his house, but she saw no signs of him.

Sighing, she started back home. When she neared the trail, she veered off toward her brother's studio.

"*Buenos noches*, Pep-squeak." Felipe stopped painting and grinned. "*Como esta?*"

"*Bien*," she murmured. She walked closer to the canvas he worked on and silently studied the bold colors. Then she shrugged. "No. I lied. I'm not fine. I've screwed up. He hates me."

His gaze narrowed, searching her face before he set his paintbrush down and wiped his hands on his shirt. "You mean Ñico?" he asked. "I wondered why he wasn't at dinner."

"I cut my hair."

"So we noticed. You look so different now." He tugged a strand and grinned. "I miss the ponytail. But it's chic. I like it."

"Ñico doesn't."

"Ah! I see the dilemma."

"It's bigger than that." Pepper sighed and plopped on a stool. Blinking back tears, she added, "He didn't want me to cut it."

"You have to admit it's a big change." He gave another gentle yank to her hair and winked. "Don't worry, Pep-squeak. He'll get used to it."

"I doubt it." Shaking her head, she tucked the same strand of hair he'd tugged behind her ear. In an effort to do something with her hands, she placed her fingers underneath her thighs. She took a deep breath and said in an offhanded manner, "Ñico no longer wants to marry me."

Felipe chuckled. "Surely you misunderstood."

"I doubt it. Ñico's words on the matter were very succinct."

He thought about this for a moment then shook his head. "That doesn't fit with what I know about Ñico. Not with his *padré* and ours pressing so hard." He gave her another considering glance, then smiled. "No. I can't believe he just withdrew like that." He snapped his fingers in the air as he spoke, then picked up his brush, ready to paint again. "Yours is too good a match. You're the perfect woman to stand by his side. There has to be more to this than a change of heart due to a haircut."

"Yes, well he's obviously changed his mind."

"Over something that will grow back?" Felipe halted in midstroke and studied her face, as if trying to fathom from her features what she was not saying. "No," he said, shaking his head once more. "You're leaving something out."

Of course there was more to it than a change of heart, but she didn't want to admit how stupid she'd been.

"Tell me what really happened. Did you push him away on purpose?" His grin was back. "Come on, Pep-squeak, confess."

She'd never been able to hold her secrets inside when he used his charm in extracting them. During her youth, Felipe had always been her confidant until differences strained their communication, and today the usual defenses she put in place because of their many disagreements disappeared. Pepper spent the next few minutes recounting her relationship with Ñico, without divulging too many intimate details.

When she finished talking, he flashed another warm smile, tugged on her hair, and said in a teasing voice that added to his actions, "Don't worry. He'll come around. He was most likely shocked." Then his smile died and his tone changed, becoming more serious. "But you need to quit playing games, *cara*. You're not being fair to Ñico. You're an adult now. Grow up and accept your responsibilities. When you sleep with him, you're committing yourself, whether you think so or not."

Pepper left her brother's studio feeling worse than when she'd entered. His chastisements had offset his words of encouragement, had in fact made her realize he didn't understand the scope of her problem. Though Felipe could be sensitive and tempestuous, he was also a male. As such, he viewed life with a masculine simplicity. Right or wrong. Black and white. No extenuating circumstances. No gray areas. What if her brother was right? Maybe it was time to grow up. Grab on to life and shape it to what she wanted. Like Second Chances. She couldn't help thinking that she'd blown this chance at love, though.

Ambling along the trail, she wandered toward the deck. Eventually, she wound her way into the living room where her mother sat with a book.

"Angelina." Elena smiled, closed the book, and set it on the table next to her. "I thought you'd be with Ñico."

"No. I'm by myself tonight." She missed his company. She didn't realize until that moment how much she'd come to depend on his steady presence each evening. He fit in so well with her family before and after dinner, laughing and joking, as if he belonged. How she wanted him to belong only to her.

"Is he working? Since he wasn't at dinner, I assumed he had pressing business."

"I'm not sure," she lied. "I don't know why he didn't show up for dinner." Pepper slumped into a chair across from Elena and sighed heavily. "No. That's not true. Oh, Mama!" A few tears broke free. She brushed them aside. Having a pity party wouldn't bring Ñico back. "I've done something terrible. I don't think he'll forgive me." Despite not wanting to give in to such emotion, more tears flooded her eyes. This time she succumbed to the impulse and let them flow.

Elena patted the seat next to her. Pepper immediately moved to the spot, while her mother slid an arm around her shoulders, squeezing gently. "Did you two have a fight?"

"No."

"No?" Grasping her shoulders, Elena leaned away. Her eyes narrowed. She searched her daughter's expression carefully before hers became more sympathetic. "Something obviously happened to have you crying." Her smile softened. "You never cry, *mi hija*."

"Maybe I've changed." She certainly didn't seem like the same woman who tended bar, fending off come-ons from tipsy tourists. Had she really been that person who used to watch old movies in her spare time? Would she ever be able to go back to her previous life?

"Change is good." Her mother opened her arms and Pepper didn't hesitate to take advantage of Elena's warmth.

"We need to talk. I think it's time you learned the truth."

"The truth?" Pepper didn't want to hear more damning proof that men couldn't change, that Ñico would never love her enough to keep from seeking out others. "Oh, Mama. What good will the truth do? Ñico is too much like Papa. I should never have fallen in love with him."

"No, *cara*, that was fate. You've loved him since you were a child. I only hope when you hear what I've done, you'll understand and not hate me."

"What do you mean? I could never hate you."

"I hope not." Elena smiled wistfully, staring off into space.

When she remained silent for too long, Pepper prodded, "Go on. I'm listening."

"Remember right before you left home, to make your escape?" At Pepper's nod she continued speaking, wringing her hands while she spoke. "I wasn't quite honest about all that had taken place. But I had my reasons."

"Oh?"

"Yes. While you were away at school, a month before you graduated, I caught Miguel flirting. At first I wasn't quite sure what to do. It had never happened before. And while I struggled to get his attention, all it really took in the end was my packing a bag with full intention of leaving. He understood then that I was serious about following through on threats I'd made years earlier. Before I married Miguel, I told him that if I ever caught wind of an affair, I would be gone within the hour. He promised me he'd never be unfaithful and I trusted his word. Miguel doesn't lie. Of course, it wouldn't do for his best friend to know the mighty Miguel Delgado was so weak as to fall in love and stay in a monogamous marriage."

Elena stopped speaking and smiled sadly. She squeezed Pepper's hand, as if she were grasping for the courage to continue. Pepper only nodded, too stunned to do much else. Why had her mother let her believe the worst?

Finally, she found her voice. "So Papa never cheated on you?"

"No, Miguel and I patched up our differences privately. I'm sorry I let you think such a thing about your father. You see, he'd never admit to giving in to my demands. He can't. He'd lose face. I don't care what the rest of the world thinks. I love him too much. I only care about what is between us."

"But why did you never tell me?"

"I had my reasons, *mi hija*, and I'm getting to them. Paulo and your father share many things. But you know men, some things they never discuss. I'm certain Paulo never knew of my ultimatum. In all our years together, Miguel had never been tempted until Mari.

She was years younger than me. I felt old and used up and so very angry. Then I found my backbone and fought. I relied on Miguel's passion and what we had together. We'd always had tremendous chemistry and thank goodness that passion never died in over twenty years. It only grew stronger."

"I still don't understand. Why would you let me think the worst of Papa?"

"For your own good."

"My own good?"

"*Sí.* I didn't want you to have to suffer like Paulo's wife did. I knew of Paulo's views and I knew his sons could only espouse the same garbage. Just the idea of Miguel looking at another woman is painful. I can easily understand why women kill unfaithful spouses."

When the pressure of Elena's fingers dug into her thigh, Pepper placed her hand over hers, offering reassurance. "It's okay, Mama. I think I'm beginning to understand."

"I was only trying to protect you. He was all you talked about," she murmured, as a tear rolled down her face. "And Ñico was taken with you back then. I saw the same glimmer of love I noted in Miguel's eyes right after we met. I fretted for years over what to do, and my worry grew as I followed his deeds while he lived with his *madré* in England. He had definitely proven to be Paulo's child, which is why I decided you mustn't marry him. He'd only make you miserable. In an effort to spare you such grief, I urged you to leave. I prayed you'd find another in Florida. But you didn't. And once I discovered he went after you with Miguel's help, my prayers changed. I prayed you'd make him work for your love, in the hopes that he'd appreciate you more." Elena gripped the hand Pepper still held. "I'm not sure if what is between you and Ñico is similar to what your father and I share, but if it is, you need to trust in love and understand fully what love means. It's a compromise. One you may have to make. I think that is what eats at you now. Do you love him?"

"Yes."

"There is nothing more potent. Use it! Be honest. Men can change. Tell him how much you care and let him know his actions can destroy your love. He needs to know the truth, and he needs to know his actions have consequences. After seeing him at dinner night after night, I believe he loves you, too. But he's a male Fernández." Elena caught her gaze, hers pleading. "Do you comprehend now why I urged you to leave?"

Pepper nodded.

"I'd hoped that somehow Ñico would realize what he'd lost and fight for you in much the same way Miguel fought for me at one time. One always appreciates something more when one earns it. I have no doubt that if you'd been here four years ago, you'd have endured years of torment. Years of uncertainty."

"I understand, Mama." She hugged Elena once more, then rose. "Thank you for telling me."

Pepper left her mother, needing to think. To absorb Elena's revelations. She dashed down the trail leading from the top of the bluff to the beach. Once her feet hit the sand, she kept to her quick pace. She didn't know how she felt. Out of balance, that was for sure, like the axis of her entire life had tilted.

Finally, she stopped and sat close to the water's edge. In the dark, looking at the waves as they crashed on the beach, her heart ached. The moon came out of hiding, spotlighting the ocean, dusting it with rays of light that glinted along with the stars above. Such a romantic setting, reminding her of the night she made love with Ñico in the water. Like the water lapping at her bare feet, the memory lapped at her senses, drawing a yearning for the man who'd come to find her in the Florida Keys. Could she trust love? Did he love her enough to change? Did she have the courage to face him and tell him her feelings? Why was love so complicated?

Chapter 14

After leaving Pepper, Ñico had driven to the other side of the island and had parked his jeep in one of his favorite spots. Hours later, he still sat staring out at the water, continuing to search the waves for the reason he felt so bereft.

He hit the steering wheel in frustration.

Why? Why should he care whether or not she cut her hair? She'd had a strong point. It was her hair. But damn it all, he'd told her how much he loved it. He'd pleaded with her to leave it alone. His pleas had not been unreasonable. Would she ever obey his pleas?

He ran a hand through his hair and rested it on his neck. He rubbed, working out the kinks. He needed to walk, to clear his mind, to push Pepper and the hurt still lurking aside.

He took off his shoes and socks. Then, after rolling his pants cuffs several times, he climbed out of the jeep and walked to the water. Only a few people lingered on the beach at this time of day. Most of the sun-worshiping tourists had moved on to the evening pleasures the island offered.

Face facts, Ñico.

He'd tried rationalization, looking for the means to ease his pain, but he was only excusing her actions. After using every excuse, he found he'd run out, and the conclusion remained constant. His wishes hadn't mattered. Not one damn bit.

Pepper should love him enough to honor his wishes.

That thought caught his attention. Where had it come from? Did he want her love? Is that what he craved?

A little girl chasing the waves almost bumped into him, pulling him out of his troubling musings. Ñico stepped out of the way, chuckling at her shy demeanor when she suddenly noticed how close she'd gotten to him. She was obviously an islander with her bronzed skin, coffee-colored eyes, and flowing ebony hair.

Birds screeched overhead. Off to the side, he noted a few fish swirling in the shallow tidal pools of the inviting blue water. The little girl ran back to her mother further down the beach. On the horizon, the sun slowly disappeared, darkening the sky to dusk. In a matter of hours, it would rise again in the east. Life went on around him.

Life. That's what he wanted. He wanted to create a life with Pepper. Children were the future. Ñico smiled, wondering at what their child might look like if they did indeed marry. Would their first be a daughter with her fiery personality? Or would they have a son with his brooding capabilities? And though he now brooded, he had to admit to feeling lighter and freer just being around Pepper. She made him laugh, made him see colors instead of merely black and white. Exactly as the nine-year-old he remembered had done when he'd been fifteen. It was that quality that drew him.

Would he ever be happy? He never thought he possessed the ability before seeking Pepper out. Not when his happiness had teetered on the edge of Paulo Fernández's rejection.

He stared at the distant ocean as thoughts of his life flashed through his mind. For as long as he could remember, he'd been focused on earning his father's acceptance, which in turn meant his love. Was it what truly mattered? Did he even care any longer? When nothing he'd done up to now appeased him? No. Not when he'd finally come to understand the truth. His *padré* would never be satisfied.

He'd have to satisfy himself.

And what would satisfy him? What did he want out of life? What did he want out of marriage?

Certainly not what his parents had.

Ñico looked up just then and saw Felipe Delgado pull into the beach parking lot.

He swore under his breath. Though he and Felipe were good friends, he damn well didn't want to have to face an inquisition right now. Not when he still wasn't sure of what he wanted.

Why couldn't the Delgado men just let him be?

"I thought I recognized the jeep." Felipe's tone was friendly, as was his smile. Tucking his hands into the pockets of his loose-fitting shorts, he turned his body toward the water before glancing over at Ñico.

The tide was coming in. Birds screeched and fish jumped. Life went on.

"Is that the only reason you stopped?" Ñico kept his gaze on a sailboat in the horizon. "Or were you looking for me specifically?"

"Why lie? I figured you'd be here as it's one of your favorite spots." He shrugged and started walking. "I had an interesting conversation with Pepper, so I decided to come to the source to see if she's being emotional, or if there is some truth to what she says."

Ñico fell into step next to him. When he didn't elaborate after walking some distance, his curiosity got the better of him, especially since Pepper's brother didn't seem ready to attack him. "Well? What was it you came to find out?"

"Did you tell her you didn't want to marry her?"

"Yes."

"Why?"

"Why?" Ñico snorted at his look of astonishment. "Why not? It's obvious she doesn't want to marry me. I got tired of fighting her."

"That's it? You're done fighting? Am I missing something?"

"Maybe, but the subject is not open for discussion." He wasn't about to share his recent musings.

"Okay. Answer me this. Did you really get upset when you saw she'd cut her hair?"

"Define upset."

"Backing out of a proposal."

Ñico remained mute, neither agreeing nor disagreeing.

"Hmmm." Felipe stopped walking and his gaze narrowed.

Ñico halted a few feet away and kept all emotion off his face.

"It did upset you. Just as she said, didn't it?" When Ñico was about to dispute this, Felipe held up a hand. "Don't bother denying the fact. I've got eyes and a mind. The truth is as easy to grasp as simple math." His smile stretched. He turned and started walking back in the direction they'd come. "I'm curious as to why a haircut would cause such a reaction."

Ñico shrugged and followed, staying silent.

"Care to tell me why? It's only hair."

"It's complicated and hard to explain." That much was the truth. "I didn't realize I wanted more."

"More? What more do you want? She's an attractive woman. You've involved her in Fernández Industries. And I know you're involved physically. What's the problem?"

"It's not enough."

"Not enough? You've called off the wedding of the year over hair? *Dios*, are you nuts?"

"Maybe. I'm still figuring it out." While he'd been staring at the water, he'd uncovered a few other revelations, one being why she'd attracted him in the first place, outside of her gorgeous body and that glorious hair. Pepper had the same spirit and sense of adventure as his mother.

"Still figuring it out? Ñico, there's nothing to figure out. Your course is set. She's the perfect heiress for you to have by your side. You'll provide for her. She'll give you children. Beautiful children, I might add."

"*Sí*. I'm well aware of her beauty." And while viewing Felipe's incredulous expression, another truth hit Ñico like a battering ram to the gut. If he married her and continued with their relationship as it was, the past had a strong chance of repeating itself. They could end up destroying everything good about what they had together just as his parents had done. His father and mother were barely civil to each other now. Even so, he had his memories of a happier couple and he'd seen earlier pictures where they had appeared in love. Where his mother smiled at his father with the same awe he'd spied in Pepper's eyes right after they'd made love.

"What about love?" he asked, parroting Pepper's question. Damn, he was going crazy. Why would he bring that up? To Pepper's brother, of all people?

Felipe stopped short, eyeing him intently. "*Dios mio*! You're in love with her, aren't you?"

"Yes—no. Hell, I don't know how I feel any longer." Did he love her? A sobering thought. But one he couldn't escape. He wiped his face before rubbing his neck and sighing. "I don't like thinking she cut her hair on purpose, to strike out at me." He had this horrible doubt, which made the pain much sharper. Did love sharpen the pain? Did Pepper love him? Was that why she wanted his fidelity...to avoid pain? Did he love her enough to give her what she wanted? "If you had asked me two weeks ago, I'd have scoffed at the thought of love. But now I can't dismiss it. I've never felt this way about anyone before."

When Felipe's smile stretched, Ñico groaned inwardly. He'd revealed too much.

"Must be my romantic side coming out, but it warms my heart to hear such sentiment coming from your lips." He clapped him on the back, still grinning as if he found Ñico's revelations highly entertaining. "I want my sister's happiness. I know Pepper loves you. She always has."

Ñico snorted. "She has a funny way of showing it."

"That's fear speaking."

"Fear?" His eyes narrowed. Though darkness had set in while they walked, overhead lights leading to the parking lot illuminated the area and he glimpsed more amusement in Felipe's expression.

"Yes. And don't look so skeptical. You were the one upset. She obviously knew what your reaction would be, so she counted on it to push you away. You made the decision for her."

"What?" He shook his head to clear it. "Wait, you lost me."

"I know Pepper. She's always spouted off about American relationships and American men. Especially after she went away to college in the States. But before that, you were all she talked about until Mama started pointing out articles in gossip magazines, which detailed your carousing in London."

Ñico sighed, rolling his eyes. "Some of those articles were gross exaggerations. I never slept with three-quarters of the women they credit to me."

"Doesn't matter. Perception is what counts. Elena verbalized her displeasure and Pepper had no choice but to listen. Yet, she never would read any of them." He snorted. "Mama went through a bit of a rebellion back then."

"Elena?" Ñico continued walking, happy to have something else to discuss besides his past misdeeds.

"Yes, Elena. I thought Papa would never get over it." Felipe grinned. "They say they are happy now. But I have to tell you, I have no intention of saddling myself with a crazy woman who expects love. You may have found it, but you, my friend, are an exception."

"I think I understand Pepper a little better now," Ñico murmured. Is that why she left the island four years ago?

Whether planned or not, Felipe's words provided an interesting insight into her motives and behavior. How would he feel if their situations had been reversed? What if she'd been the one with the past lovers, and what if she'd stated she couldn't remain faithful?

Just the thought of another man touching what he considered his had his pulse pounding and his temperature spiking. Ñico clenched a fist, stifling the urge to hit something. More insight. How had he been so stupid not to see it? What's more, he realized just then, he had no desire to conquer other women. Hell, he'd long outgrown that useless endeavor in London. From the moment he first laid eyes on Pepper again, he'd thought of no one but her. No woman had ever brought forth the drive to work at melding her into his life, something she'd resisted at all levels, which only had him increasing his efforts. Now that he was so close to victory, he couldn't back down.

Whether she knew it or not, she was his.

"If you love her, tell her so."

"Oh?" Ñico quirked an eyebrow at Felipe and grinned. "Why should I listen to your advice? Especially when, by your own admission, love is something you don't believe in and are avoiding at all costs?"

"My cynicism isn't the dilemma." By this point they'd returned to where they'd started. "I stand by my advice," Felipe said. "Talk to her. Tell her how you feel. It's the only way to smooth this over."

In due time, Ñico thought, nodding. First he planned on making sure she realized what he had just discovered. They belonged together. They always had and they always would.

He and Felipe walked in the direction of the parked cars. He climbed into his jeep at the same time Felipe entered his car, waving good-bye.

Ñico headed in the opposite direction. He wasn't going home just yet. He had one stop to make.

He swung into the drive leading to Paulo Fernández's palatial estate.

In seconds he let himself in the front door, nodding to the servant who rushed to greet him.

"Good evening. It's nice to see you, *señor*. Can I get you anything?" he asked, following Ñico as he moved through the Spanish-tiled entry with quick steps.

"I'm looking for my *padré*." He glanced into the library before checking the formal living room. Both rooms were vacant. "Have you seen him?"

"He's out on the patio."

"*Gracias*," Ñico said, striding for the French doors leading to the well-lit outside terrace.

He spotted his father sitting at a wrought iron table, reading a newspaper.

When he approached, Paulo folded the paper in deliberate moves and set it aside.

"Ñico. Have you come to share the news of your impending wedding?"

"I've news, but I'm not sure you'll like what I have to say." He sat down across from him, holding his gaze steady.

"Oh?"

"Our wedding is off."

"What?"

"I said, our—"

"I heard you the first time," Paulo yelled. "What the hell is wrong with you? She's a Delgado. She's my choice."

"I'm well aware of your views. Now I'm stating mine. I've decided I want more out of life than pleasing you."

"You've decided?" His father's gaze narrowed and he studied his face as if the meaning of his news was typed there in fine print. "When did you come to this *decision*?"

Ñico stretched and couldn't stop the smile that snuck forth. "Actually, it's been a work in progress." Who knew he'd find his father's reaction so amusing. Did the old man think Ñico would forever beg for his attention and good graces?

His grin expanded. Of course he did. Well, it was time to become an adult and face facts. Those good graces were always just out of reach, much like the bunny greyhounds chased. The only difference? The greyhounds caught one now and then to reinforce the behavior. Paulo would never allow him to catch his goodwill.

His favor would always be inches out of reach.

"I've decided a few other things, too." Ñico sighed. Might as well be honest. "I have no wish to follow in your footsteps, Papa. I don't want your legacy."

"And what legacy would that be?"

"One of enduring battles of wills until all love is slashed to shreds."

"Bah! You're talking riddles." Paulo waved off his reply. "The only legacy I've wished to pass on is for you to be a man like your brother Juan."

"I'm not Juan, Papa. I can't take his place." Ñico shrugged, not allowing the dig to derail his honesty. "And if becoming a man means living in his shadow, then I'll never be one. Nor am I proud of using coercion, hoping to manipulate Pepper into marriage for only your approval. No matter what I do, I'll never have it. Pepper's happiness is my new focus." His voice hardened as well as his resolve. He leaned forward and hit his fist, emphasizing his point. "That is why I decided if we marry, the choice will be hers. I love her. More than life itself. And even though I want marriage more than anything, I won't use your tactics. I won't force her." It would mean nothing if he did. He realized that now. Ñico discovered something else in those few seconds. Saying what he really felt was cathartic. Why stop now? He should get it all out before he left.

He stood and waited for Paulo's complete attention. "And for your information, I am a man. I've achieved much in my life. If you'd only open your eyes and quit comparing me to my dead brother, you'd see *me*! You'd also see I'm not my mother." He shook his head and his tone saddened. "Your opinion has always mattered. Until today. I simply don't care how you judge me anymore."

He turned to leave, but his father's voice stopped him.

"Ñico! *Un minuto, por favor.*"

Pivoting, Ñico inhaled a deep breath, preparing for a harsh retort. More disapproval. Maybe he hadn't been totally honest, but he'd never let Paulo see how his actions could still affect him. His chin rose. "*Sí?*"

"You're a wiser man than I was at your age," his father said, rising from the table and moving toward him with an outstretched hand. "I'm a fool not to have noticed the fact before now."

Hesitantly, Ñico reached out. The second their hands met, he was pulled into a bear hug he hadn't expected. His father leaned away grinning, and clapped him on the back. His next words shocked the hell out of him.

"You're right. You've definitely earned my respect these past four years. What's more, you're a better man for putting me in my place." Paulo met his gaze and added earnestly, "I wish you a happy life." Then Ñico spied something he never thought to glimpse in his father's eyes. Admiration, highlighted with regret. "I admit to making a few huge mistakes in my life. The biggest one was losing your mother. Every time I look into your face, I'm reminded of my stupidity. I'm sorry for making you pay for my failure. Follow your heart, my son. Grab on to this woman who holds your love and never let her go."

"*Gracias*, Papa." Ñico nodded, feeling ten feet tall. In all his thirty-one years, he'd never heard such warm words from Paulo Fernández. He gave his father a heartfelt hug. "*Te quiero*," he whispered, suddenly overwhelmed with emotion. He did love his father.

"*Sí, te quiero, mi hijo.*"

It felt good and made him realize they'd come to some kind of understanding in these last minutes. It was amazing how a few sentences and complete candor could change an outlook.

Now if he could somehow follow his father's advice and grab on to Pepper without her batting him away, he'd be the happiest man in the universe.

Ñico drove home. He walked through his house, feeling lonely. Thoughts of the last time she'd been in these rooms filled him. He couldn't get the scent of her out of his nostrils, nor could he forget the way she'd belonged here. In his home. There was no other woman for him. She was his soul mate. He should have recognized the fact the moment he met her again. He'd never find another woman more vibrant, more passionate, more suited to him than her. Why would he ever seek anyone else?

The rooms closed in, squeezing the air from his lungs. He couldn't breathe; he needed space. Ñico headed for the water, then turned and walked in the direction of the Delgado residence.

~

"I've been looking for you."

Pepper turned away from the water at Ñico's voice and face him. "Why?" Though she'd planned to blurt out her honest feelings, suddenly her courage deserted her. She wasn't quite sure what she'd do if he laughed at her confession of love or twisted it for his own purposes.

"We need to talk. Will you walk with me for a bit, *querida*?"

"Sure." She stood when he got closer and took his offered hand. The fact that he'd used the endearment was a good sign.

He continued walking at a slow pace near the water's edge, seeming lost in thought.

The two walked a quarter of a mile before Pepper's curiosity overcame her hesitancy. "Well?" she asked softly. "I thought you wanted to talk. Have you changed your mind?" She prayed the answer would be yes.

"About our paths being different?" When she nodded, Ñico shook his head. "No. I meant what I said."

Regret filled her, but she still managed a weak smile. "Won't your father be disappointed?"

He stopped and eyed her cautiously. "His disappointment no longer matters." In a heartbeat, her noble Spaniard had vanished. In his place was merely a man who'd told her he loved her hair and had pleaded with her not to cut it. The pain etched into his expression tore at her heart. Pepper knew then that somehow she had hurt him, and if she could undo her actions, she would.

"I'm sorry I cut my hair, Ñico. You were right. I did it because you asked me not to. I'm so sorry."

Ñico shoved a hand into his pocket and looked out at the water, still holding on to her hand with the other. "I have my own reasons for sorrow." He turned back to her, his gaze searching, and brought her fingers to his lips. "I've been thinking and have come to a few conclusions, but before I get to them. I have one question. And I'd like an honest answer."

"Okay."

"Why did you run from me?"

"You mean four years ago?"

He nodded.

Pepper chewed on her bottom lip, studying his grave expression. She wasn't sure she could divulge her deepest insecurities, but she didn't see how she could avoid doing so.

"It's a silly reason." When Ñico's eyebrows rose and he waited patiently for her to continue, she gave him a sad smile and told him the truth. "I thought you'd forgotten me." This time, she was the one who glanced at the water, unable to keep meeting his intense gaze. "I was sure I could never measure up to all those beautiful, worldly women you found so fascinating in London." She offered a half shrug. "So I ran." Finally, she had to ask her own question. "Why didn't you wait for me?"

"I have no excuse, except stupidity." He exhaled. His fingers moved to her hair, where he tucked a few blowing strands behind her ear. "I'm one of those who had to find out the truth the hard way."

"I'm sure not many would consider womanizing in such terms."

He chuckled. "I prefer to think I had to experience my share of shallow creatures in order to appreciate a rare jewel."

"I see. Kind of like a woman kissing a lot of frogs before she meets her prince?"

"That's a nicer way of explaining my actions." Ñico nodded. "I have no idea why I thought I needed to clutter my life with such baubles, when I knew you were waiting."

"Hmm. A rare jewel? I rather like the description. Is that really how you see me?"

"Yes." The back of his hand brushed her face. "Are you sorry you haven't kissed any other frogs?"

"Mercy, no. Why would I be? I recognized my prince when I was nine years old." Pepper took a deep breath for courage and added, "I've loved him for all these years. And I waited for him. I knew he'd come for me eventually." Her grin widened. "Of course he became a big frog in the meantime."

"One kiss from you changed me." He laughed, wrapped his hand around her neck, and pulled her closer. "No way I could remain a frog after that kiss. I love you, *querida*. Marry me and make me the happiest man in the world. Let me make it up to you for being such a toad."

"I thought we were taking different paths."

"This is a different path. The old one led to heartache. The path I want now is commitment. I don't want any other woman. Ever." His head lowered, and right before his lips met hers, he said, "I love you, Pepper Delgado. I'll never stop loving you and if you marry me, I'll spend the rest of my life proving my love."

Ñico broke the connection and got down on one knee. "Will you marry me?"

Pepper smiled. "I thought you'd never ask."

About the Author

Sandy Loyd is a Western girl through and through. Born and raised in Salt Lake City, she's worked and lived in some fabulous places in the US, including Arizona, Northern California and South Florida. She now resides in Kentucky and writes full time. As much as she loves her current hometown, she misses the mountains and has to go back to her roots to get her mountain fix at least once a year.

She believes our country is immensely diverse and she has lived in some great places and has much fodder to write about.

She spent her single years in San Francisco and considers that city one of America's treasures, comparable to no other city in the world. Sandy also spent a decade in South Florida, diving, sailing and enjoying other activities on the water. Tropical Spice is set in the Florida Keys.

Check out her website at **www.sandyloyd.com** for dates of Rachael and Karen's stories the second and third in the Second Chances Series.

Like her on Facebook **www.facebook.com/sloydwrites** and she'll keep you updated as to releases or follow her on Twitter **www.twitter.com/sloydwrites**

Another city Sandy loves is Washington D.C. With all the museums and history, our nation's capital is like no other. Her D.C. Badboys Series, beginning with The Sin Factor, set in the D.C. area, are mystery/suspense stories full of twists that keep the reader guessing, along with a few harrowing scenes and of course, a heartwarming love story. The characters are fun, normal people who are trying to get by, just like people everywhere.

Below is an excerpt of **The Sin Factor:**

Chapter 1

Tree branches swayed, bending to the will of a brisk breeze. Dusk prevailed—that moment in time when it was neither dark nor light.

Avery Montgomery slowly turned to peer at the surrounding landscape, scrutinizing the trees and brush to her left and directly behind her where the gravesites ended. In front of her and still visible in the twilight row after row of pearly headstones fanned out in precise lines.

Shivering, she rubbed her arms.

She waited.

As if her thoughts had ordered the air to still, the leaves stopped their movement. For endless minutes all was calm, until a prickly sensation at the back of her neck indicated his presence, a feeling she'd had before.

Every nerve ending in her body stood at alert. Still waiting. For what, she had no idea.

She closed her eyes and chastised herself. After all, she stood in a cemetery—Arlington, at that. She took a deep breath. The smell of fresh-cut grass eased the eeriness of standing so close to the remains of dead soldiers.

Yet, the feeling of being watched didn't dissipate. Did he realize she sensed him watching? Why assume it was a he? She pretended not to notice. If she pretended hard enough, then *he* wasn't real. Pretending had become a huge part of her life in recent years. She had no reason to doubt her pretense wouldn't work. It had all those other nights she'd stood staring at the graves of two men who'd died almost two months ago.

Avery's focus returned to the headstones. She concentrated on the chiseled words.

Major Michael Andrew Montgomery.

Major Marshall Compton Crandall.

One had been her husband for most of her adult life and the other had been his best friend. Both died serving their country, a sacrifice honored with an Arlington burial.

She glanced toward the heavens. If only she could go back in time and undo her past. Unfortunately, it was written, never to be undone, and she would have to live with the consequences.

"You look so sad."

She pivoted and leaned toward the voice. The soft sound penetrated her ears and reached into her soul, as if directed solely, intimately to her. Squinting, she could only see shadows of trees in the now moonlit darkness.

Ignore it. It isn't real.

Avery shrugged it off and sighed. She was obviously hallucinating. She stood alone in the middle of a cemetery, and cemeteries were notorious for evoking weird feelings.

"I guess I am sad," she whispered, going against her mind's reasoning because she felt compelled to answer. Oh dear God. She was going crazy. Why did she have this overwhelming need to hear his voice again? Avery's narrowed gaze searched the darkened brush once more. She spent a moment listening. When no other noise sounded, she turned back to the two graves.

In seconds, tears emerged, and it dawned on her that she *was* sad…grief-stricken…for what would never be…for what her transgressions had manifested.

"I'm so sorry, Mike. I never meant to make such a mess of things." More tears trickled. Her husband had gone to his grave with no other word than the confusing letter he'd sent right before he died. She'd never know if he'd forgiven her or not.

Stop it. It's too late for forgiveness.

She wiped away her tears.

A ping sounded a few feet away. In the next instant, a force hit her from behind, throwing her off balance. Her legs buckled from the weight. Too stunned to do anything but put out her hands to soften the fall, she hit the ground with a hard thud.

"*Oomph,*" she cried out none too gracefully as the air escaped her chest. She slowly gained her wits and tried to move, but couldn't. Something…or someone…hampered her. A man. He rolled with her, using the headstones as a shield. A chunk of earth bounced off the ground only inches away and she identified the ping.

"My God! Those are bullets." Arms flailing, she struggled to get up.

"Stay down," he said, his voice low but urgent.

She couldn't do much else with the man sprawled on top of her. She recognized her figment's voice. A living, breathing human voice.

"This is Arlington," she whispered, fighting to rein in her out-of-control imagining of a gun-toting terrorist hiding in the bushes taking potshots. "Why is someone shooting?"

~

Jeffrey Sinclair caught the panic in her voice. "I don't know why, but I intend to find out." He shifted and covered her more protectively. Through layers of clothes, he felt her heartbeat race. Or was it his?

He managed to yank his radio out of his pocket and hit the button just as another bullet ricocheted off a headstone to his left. "Three shots fired." With his lips next to her ear, he kept his voice low. "As far as I can tell, from northwest of my position."

"On it," came the reply.

Silence prevailed. In those quiet seconds, the alert edge left his body in an exhale, but she remained as immobile as stone.

"You're safe," he assured her in a soothing tone. "I won't let anything happen to you." Sin wasn't the protecting type, but as the promise escaped his lips, he realized he meant every word.

She nodded and seemed to relax a bit. Her lemony scent blended with the dampened earth and invaded his nostrils. An inconvenient blast of awareness shot through him. As the danger diminished with each passing minute, leftover adrenaline had his heartbeat quickening, pumping more alertness through every vein and artery. He felt trapped in some kind of suspended time warp, intensifying the craziness of lying prone over some stranger. Well, not exactly a stranger. He knew enough, and though he couldn't deny an attraction to her, he damn sure hadn't expected Avery Montgomery to affect him like this.

Hold it together, Sin.

Remember why you're on top of her in the first place. Someone shot at her. Unfortunately, his mental commands couldn't extinguish her warmth radiating beneath him. The hard contours of his body dug into her softness, adding to his awareness…and his discomfort. He closed his eyes, willing Des to hurry, and forced himself to relax. To keep breathing.

Five…ten…twenty seconds ticked by and still nothing happened.

Finally, he lifted off her enough to let her roll onto her back but he wouldn't relinquish his protective posture. Damn. Not his smartest move because now she lay underneath him face up. Darkness obscured her full features, but he didn't need to see her to know she was gorgeous.

The rapid thumping of his heart continued to override the silence. With her head inches from his, the soft air of her even breathing caressed his neck. His blood pounded faster.

Don't think about it. Think about the situation. Where in the hell is Des?

Finally, the radio came alive again. "All clear. Whoever was shooting is long gone. I'll scout around a little more, see what I can find."

"Thanks, but be careful. It ruins my night when someone uses me for target practice," he answered.

Sin pushed up onto his forearms and looked down to see Avery suck in air and open her eyes. At the same time, the full moon came out of hiding and a bit of light reflected off her face, highlighting a frightened brown gaze. He began to pull away, but the glimpse of sadness he also saw stopped him cold. For long seconds their stares locked. Peering into such vivid, expressive eyes was the wrong thing to do, but he couldn't look away.

Her turbulent gaze spoke volumes, created a bond of sorts. A *mental connection*, for lack of a better term, that was damned unwelcome and tossed his thoughts into chaos. Questions that had rested on the tip of his tongue scattered to the far reaches of his mind.

Whoever said the eyes were the windows to the soul had it right. He didn't know her—they'd never met—but it was as if he'd known her forever. How stupid was that? Or maybe surreal. This entire scene had a dream-like quality to it.

Of its own accord, his gaze dropped inches lower, to her mouth. An incredibly beautiful mouth. He certainly wasn't considering doing something so stupid like kissing that mouth, was he? Yeah, because even as his brain shouted no, his body had other ideas. At that point, stupid just didn't seem to matter.

In slow motion, he lowered his head, giving her plenty of time to turn away.

Avery didn't move, yet that expressive gaze seemed to beg him for something, which spurred him to continue. She still didn't pull away even when his mouth hovered over hers before grazing back and forth. The not quite kisses sent searing flashes of heat straight through him. When her lips connected with his, he wrapped his arms around her in an effort to bring her closer. Never had a kiss seemed so elemental…like breathing. Like being in heaven.

"I don't see any shell casings. I'm betting the bullets came from a high-powered rifle," his radio squawked. "So, I'll try to find the bullets."

Instantly, he broke the kiss and felt a twinge of regret.

Whether it was for the interruption or his impulsive act, he wasn't certain.

~

As the voice seeped into Avery's thoughts, reality hit. Her entire body stiffened. Panic re-entered her consciousness, along with total embarrassment, as the reason she lay underneath a stranger in a cemetery in the first place returned. Someone had shot at her. She had to get out of here. Get home and make sure her son was okay.

"Sin?" the same voice asked. "You there?"

He lifted off her and said into his radio, "I'm here," then rolled away to say more.

Sin? Was that his name? How fitting. He truly was some specter sent from hell to torment her. She wasn't someone who rolled around in graveyards with strange men after being shot at. She was a grieving widow. A mother, for heaven's sake. Didn't she have enough to feel guilty over?

"Are you okay?"

She glanced up at the sound and caught him eyeing her with concern etched into his expression. *Are you okay? Question of the year.* No, she was not okay. She'd never be okay. To prove it, she'd just spent the last few minutes in mindless absurdity, wishing the kiss with a complete stranger could go on forever. She nodded and worked at pretending she wasn't staring into the most incredible gaze, one that saw more than she cared to expose.

Avery rubbed her temples. Who the hell was he? Whoever he was, he'd probably saved her life. Risking another glance, she took a deep breath. Even in the shadows, she noted an arresting presence. His face wasn't pretty. Too many angles and hard edges…adding to his undeniable maleness. And he had a power about him that held her in its force, which only increased her internal turbulence. No wonder she'd felt protected underneath him and totally safe, which made no sense at all.

In the blink of an eye, her fear returned full force. She was totally aware of her vulnerability. His size, dwarfing her five feet nine inches, suddenly made her feel defenseless.

"You sure?" He waited a moment, watching her closely. When she didn't offer a reply, he stood, bent to help her, and flashed a quick, lopsided grin. "Sorry about that kiss. I got carried away."

Avery took his offered hand and allowed him to pull her up. "I…um…no problem." What else could she say? She'd gotten carried away too? He probably thought kissing men she'd never met in cemeteries after being shot at was her norm.

Someone shot at her.

"I need to go." She yanked her hand out of his grasp. *Home.* Everything would be okay if she could just make it home and check on Andy. That thought became a driving force.

"Hold on." He reached for his wallet, retrieved a business card, and held it out. "My name's Jeffrey Sinclair."

Avery stopped her retreat long enough to take the card.

So his name was Sinclair, not Sin. The fact didn't ease her conscience any after what she'd just done. Sin or no Sin, she'd made a complete fool of herself. She had to get out of here.

Despite a million questions peppering her brain just then, she turned and darted out of instinct, disturbed by the kiss as much as what preceded it.

Never in a billion years would she consider herself someone who'd meet an unknown man's mouth so crazily. Not when, according to Mike, she was frigid and never got emotional. But here she was an emotional mess and the thought only swamped her with more emotion.

She veered in the direction of her parked car as more

humiliation rose up over her reaction to a complete stranger. His presence had made her feel cherished. That alone seemed totally illogical, but when he'd bent to kiss her, she hadn't been able to turn away. In those few seconds she'd felt more alive than she had in fifteen years. Mike's kisses had never generated such a response.

"Wait. I'd like to talk to you. Make sure you're safe."

That same gripping, almost disturbing voice carried on the wind. She fought to ignore the urgent tone, but somehow the quality reached past the physical, just as his concerned stare had done, touching something deep inside of her she didn't want touched.

"No…" she said over her shoulder. "I'm fine. Really. I appreciate your help, but I've got to get home." By the time she made it to her car she was running. She slowed her steps and looked back. He'd made no attempt to follow, thank God, just stood and watched her in the moonlit shadows. With her focus still on him, she hit the keyless entry. Lights flashed and the locks snapped up. She scrambled inside.

In seconds, Avery had her seat belt fastened and the car started. She worked to keep her foot steady as she put the car in gear and sped off.

Maybe running away denoted cowardice, but cowardice was the least of her troubles.

~

"What happened? Why is she leaving?"

Jeffrey Sinclair ignored the questions, still keeping a protective watch as her car's taillights flashed brighter when she slowed to turn left onto the main road leading out of the cemetery.

"Sin?" Desmond Phillips strode up to him. "Why didn't you stop her?"

He turned to his business partner and grunted. "She's not going anywhere."

"But it's obvious at this point she's part of it. She's been here every night we've staked out the gravesite. This would've been the perfect opportunity to discover what she knows."

"It can wait. What I want to know is…why would someone try and kill her?"

"Diversionary tactic," Des spit out. "Had to be. A high-powered rifle with a silencer? He was probably using a scope. Had a clean shot and missed. On purpose. To draw us out. Which in my book indicates some kind of involvement."

"Maybe." Sin's gaze moved to the now empty street. He clenched a fist, hating that he had no answers. Why had he spoken to her? Even more disturbing, why had he kissed her…her, of all women?

He snorted. Hell, he knew why. He hadn't been able to stop, that's why. Now, more than ever, she intrigued him. Each and every evening she'd made her nightly visits, he'd stationed himself just feet away. Watching…waiting…wanting.

"Shit," he whispered, then shook his head. Why deny his attraction? She was one gorgeous woman with curves in all the right places. He'd dealt with attraction before and never lost his head. Not like tonight, when she'd seemed so forlorn, peering at him with those haunting eyes, begging him to give in to the need.

Sin's fingernails dug deeper into his palms to the point of pain. He needed to find out if a connection existed between his company's stolen technology and the two dead Army officers. He couldn't let attractive females sidetrack him. As Des said, the lady now appeared to be involved. But to what extent?

"It's a waste of time to keep watching tonight. Nothing's going to happen now."

Des' voice yanked him back to the the reason they were lurking in a cemetery—the anonymous tip concerning the thefts from Sinclair Phillips & Coleman Electronics. "I agree." He nodded. "Whoever we were waiting for most likely got scared off with all the commotion."

"Had to be a setup." Des flashed a light onto the grass surrounding the headstones. The light caught something shiny. He stopped, then crouched and dug at the ground with his pocketknife.

"But why?" Sin drew a hand through his hair before resting it on the back of his neck. He began rubbing, trying to massage the kinks out. "What the hell have we stumbled into? Nothing makes sense. It's as if someone's playing a sick game. With our company. With our livelihood." The last phase of testing SPC's prototypes had been right on schedule until they'd gone missing. Now they had to deal with two more thefts.

"According to Colonel Williams' report, neither Major Crandall nor Major Montgomery fit the traitor profiles, and there's nothing to show their involvement." He watched Des extract a bullet from a nearby tree. Yet Montgomery had been in charge of testing the powerful light-driven tracking, listening, and recording devices. The dead major was the last known person to have them in his possession. In an attempt to learn all he could about him…and about *her*, Sin had memorized the pertinent details.

The stunning brunette's life read like a storybook romance on paper until Montgomery's death. Her deceased husband had been an all-American—athletic, good-looking, gifted—the poster boy for his college fraternity. The high school sweethearts had lived in the D.C. area, attending local Alexandria schools until college. He'd been two years ahead of her, graduating *summa cum laude* from Georgetown University before entering the Army.

"The colonel's right. Major Montgomery served ten years with a spotless record and several medals." Sin exhaled a resigned sigh. "He's a fricking war hero, not your usual scumbag who's sold his country's latest technology to the highest bidder."

Crandall's file read similarly. Despite the glowing words, Sin wasn't about to remove either officer from his short list of suspects. Military Intelligence had cleared them of all wrongdoing, but he and his partners couldn't afford to overlook any possibility. Too much was at stake.

"Maybe Montgomery needed the money."

"Money wasn't an issue." Sin met Des' gaze. "He came from old money, had access to a hefty trust fund. In fact, according to the file, several generations of Montgomerys earned money through interest, not hard work, and they all had one thing in common. They believed in giving back to society through public service, which plays into the war hero scenario."

He didn't want to think he harbored a prejudice toward dead heroes, but if Sin were totally honest, he'd have to admit to one. He'd always held such men in contempt, those born with not only the silver spoon but also the whole meal.

"Crandall didn't have Montgomery's megabucks, but their backgrounds are parallel." Sin scrubbed a hand over his face. How could they be anything but heroes with that upbringing? Poster boys like Montgomery always had it easy, had their way paved, so much so they never had to truly fight for anything, always got their pick of everything just because of who they were…the best jobs with the best salaries attracting the best mates. The gutter Sin had climbed out of was totally at the other end of the spectrum. Unlike Montgomery or Crandall, he'd had to fight for everything.

Still, he dealt in logic and probabilities. Logically, the probabilities pointed to their innocence. As the colonel had stated during their last meeting, they had nil to go on as far as motive for tying either man to any treasonous treachery.

"The wife's involved. I know it. She's been here every night we have." Des pocketed the bullets and was now shining the light in the distance. "That means something."

"Coincidence. She *is* Montgomery's widow, after all."

"Too much coincidence for my liking. Who visits a gravesite so often these days?" Des' voice held disbelief. "And for so long?"

"A grieving widow whose husband recently died?"

"Maybe." Des nodded, still searching. "Or maybe she's in on it and the husband wasn't?"

Sin's gaze followed the beam of light hitting row after row of white stones. "She's definitely someone to question, but you can't really think she's involved in passing stolen technology?"

168

"I'm suspicious of everyone until I understand their motives," Des said. "If she were the target tonight, she'd be dead. And since she was alive enough to run away, my gut tells me she's part of the ploy to draw us out."

"You're too cynical. I'd think you'd be less biased, given your previous occupation," Sin teased. Such scorn resulted from Des' colossal mistake—marrying the wrong woman. Sin understood because he hadn't made the best of choices in a wife and had his own form of cynicism in dealing with the opposite sex. Still, he tried to be objective about it.

"Cynical or not, she's someone I want to interrogate." Des flicked off the light, but not before Sin caught the annoyance on his face.

Yep, Des' expression and tone indicated he'd already tried and convicted the lady. Sin wasn't inclined to condemn her so hastily. She just didn't seem like the traitor type. Having never finished her degree, she'd dropped out to marry Montgomery ten years ago and had a baby some seven months after the wedding.

Okay, so they had to get married, Sin thought. But that was kids being too hot and heavy and not using birth control. As far as he was concerned, being stupid and horny rarely led to selling out your country for monetary gain. He could even see how it might have happened, given Avery was a woman a man could lose his sanity over enough to forget the condom.

Lucky bastard…then again, maybe not so lucky as the guy's ashes are buried only two feet away and she's still vibrantly alive. If she were his, he wouldn't want to be separated from her for an instant.

"There has to be something," he whispered, not liking the ditch his thoughts had plowed into. "Some link with her dead husband to all of this."

"The wife *is* the connection, I'm telling you." Des pointed his flashlight at him as if making a point. "Wives, especially wives who've been married for so long, generally know not only where the bodies are buried, but how many and how deep."

Sin didn't reply. Right now the widow was the only solid

lead they had.

"What about Williams? Maybe the military's made progress."

Sin frowned. "I doubt it." Colonel Williams was the Army official in charge of procuring and, in his mind, the person who supposedly got things done. Yet their Army liaison seemed useless in this situation. "He's not concerned with the theft, thanks to the fail-safe." If the prototypes landed in the wrong hands, they'd shut down without the proper sequence of numbers, and then self-destruct in fifteen hundred hours. Roughly seven days from now unless reactivated. "I rushed through the process and finalized our contract with the Army without thoroughly weighing the consequences. I certainly didn't think anyone would steal our product before it'd been fully tested." Sin sighed. "I thought the military would provide an element of security."

"It's understandable." Des clapped him on the back and grinned. "If you can't trust your government, who can you trust?"

"That's no excuse." Sin clenched his jaw. "Not for us. Not for me. Fulfilling this contract is too essential to our success." If the components weren't found in time, Williams would declare the project a failure. SPC Electronics, would be out millions, a loss they couldn't afford right now. Due to a provision in the contract stating SPC would be paid only upon confirmation of the technology working, there wasn't a damned thing Sin could do to stop the verdict.

"It's obvious the colonel has little interest in helping us." Sin shook his head in frustration. "He doesn't give a shit about whether or not we go under. His main concerns are saving face and not having to deal with military bureaucracy." With only a week left, the clock was ticking.

"I've still got a few friends on the force who owe me some favors." Des started walking toward the road. "I'll see if they can analyze these bullets." He patted his pocket. "Maybe we'll learn something useful."

Sin nodded and silently fell into step. At least Williams had provided him with a special sticker, the same one surviving spouses and family members received to enter the national cemetery after hours. "Maybe we should reconsider hiring a PI."

"We don't need outsiders." Des exhaled heavily. "They hold too many risks."

Sin nodded. Trust was the biggest issue, that and finding an investigator with the clearances necessary to deal with such sensitive information

"You're right, of course," Sin finally said, as they reached his car. When Des sent him a questioning look, he added, "We should talk to Mrs. Montgomery, and the sooner the better. Let's go back to the office to see if Eric's still there." Eric Coleman was their third partner.

He hit the keyless entry. Both opened their doors and slid inside simultaneously.

Sin wasn't looking forward to questioning the lady, given his earlier reaction. Maybe Des could do it without him. The minute the thought was out, he discarded it.

An ex-homicide detective, Des could spot inconsistencies and lies within seconds of talking to a person, a handy skill to possess due to the sensitive nature of their business. He was also a real pro at solving puzzles, but his friend wasn't what Sin would call a people person. With his square, muscular physique, he'd make a perfect bouncer in one of D.C.'s hottest nightclubs. And despite his stern, military-like bearing and short, dirty-blond buzz cut, both throwbacks from an early Marine Corps experience, the ladies must like him as he never lacked female company.

Sin watched Des snap his seat belt into place. Smiling, he started the engine and pulled onto the road. As he drove, his grin spread. He stifled a chuckle. Since Sin had already irritated the female in question with his actions, he couldn't risk poking the stick of Des' contemptuous personality at her and inflaming her further. SPC's chief of security might attract women like pollen-loaded daisies attracted bees, but his demeanor toward them was spiked with vinegar, not honey.

Questioning Mrs. Montgomery required teamwork, and they made a great team…sort of like good cop/bad cop when they interviewed prospective employees and clients.

Sin's breath came out in a long sigh. Unfortunately, he'd have to play his good cop part if he wanted to gain any useful information.

The memory of having her soft body under his flashed and he shifted uncomfortably on the leather seat.

"Damn," he said under his breath, punching the accelerator. No matter how hard he tried, the image wouldn't shake free. He didn't need any more complications.

And Avery Montgomery might prove to be a huge one.

~

Once Avery was miles down the road, well away from *him*, the incident replayed in her mind. *Incident?* She snorted, unable to describe what happened so simply.

An out-of-control kiss, maybe, but definitely not a mere incident. Guilt immersed her, filling her with more self-loathing. How could she have acted like a complete idiot…a lovesick fool without any restraint? She was a grieving widow, not some sex-starved hussy.

If that were true, then why did some part of her wonder what would have happened if they hadn't been interrupted? No. She hadn't liked kissing him. Fear, grief, and remorse had hit her all at once, creating her erratic behavior. Even so, she had to admit that Mike's kisses had never affected her like that.

At a red light, she closed her eyes for a brief second. Without the man's influence, she could finally think clearer. Someone had shot at her. Her earlier fear returned full force. Ice water ran through her veins replacing some of the other emotions. She stared in the rearview mirror searching for unseen threats and making note of those behind her.

When the light changed, her foot pushed the gas pedal. Hard.

The car shot forward and sped up quickly. Her eyes kept checking the rearview mirror as she drove. One car in particular caught and held her attention. Her heartbeat increased.

Avery breathed out a relieved sigh the moment the car turned off, blocks from her house.

She pressed the garage door opener so that it was fully open when she pulled into her driveway at the rear of her Georgetown house. She didn't wait to hit the button to lower the door. As it closed, she put the car in park, turned off the engine, and stared at the wall in front of her.

Maybe she should have gone to the police. No. Arlington was military jurisdiction and she'd rather avoid anything to do with the military, especially Colonel Williams. She didn't fully trust him. Yet, what about the guy she'd kissed? Who was he?

Her hand went to her pocket, where she'd stashed his business card. She pulled it out and read: *Jeffrey Sinclair—CEO of SPC Electronics*. He said he wanted to talk to her. What was he doing at the gravesite, and not just tonight? She had no doubt he'd been there on those other nights she'd visited. And her biggest concern…who was shooting and why? Was she the target or was *he*?

Had to be him. And I got caught in some kind of crossfire.

Movement at the door separating the kitchen and the garage drew Avery's attention and Terry poked her head out after opening it.

Her sister watched for several minutes before she stepped forward and smiled. "Everything okay?" she asked, opening the car door when Avery made no attempt to move.

Avery couldn't help but notice how close the question was to what *he* had asked. As far as she was concerned, the answer hadn't changed. She wondered if she'd ever be *okay* again. She sighed, tucked the card away, intending to research the company later, and climbed out of the car.

"Sure." She returned the smile. Except it felt forced. Without meeting Terry's curious gaze, she grabbed her purse and headed inside. She needed to think…analyze her behavior…before she told anyone about the events of the past hour, and that included her sister.

The minute Avery got through the door, her son rushed her, extracting a more natural grin. It was hard not to smile when Andy was around.

"Hey, kiddo!" She ruffled his hair before wrapping her arms around him as he hugged her waist. She walked further into the kitchen without breaking contact. "You have school in the morning. Shouldn't you be in bed?"

"I was too scared to go to bed alone. Aunt Terry said I could wait up for you."

Avery hugged her son more fiercely. "Sorry I wasn't here, honey."

"That's okay. But I'll be able to sleep if you tuck me in."

Andy didn't wait for an answer, instead went skipping off toward his room with absolute conviction she would follow. Avery did, relieved he was so resilient, and wishing she could steal some of his resiliency. If only her mind worked like a child's, then she could forget the past and bounce back, ready to tackle the next phase of her life. Like a mantle, the shadow of her deeds fell on her shoulders again, weighing her down like the heaviest stones.

When she entered her son's room, Avery found him under the blanket, holding up a book and watching her with hopeful expectation. She grinned and strode toward him, unable to deny his unspoken request. Manipulated or not, she was a sucker for Andy's sweet expression.

She slid in next to him, got comfortable, and pulled him closer. With him curled beside her, she opened the book and began reading. Ten minutes later, she unwound herself from his slumbering form, careful not to wake him.

Avery stood and stared at her son's features, so much like Mike's. Raw pain gripped her, held her in its clutches, and ripped her heart in two. Andy was the spitting image of her husband at the same age. She had the many pictures in albums to prove it. Was this her punishment…to be haunted by her actions every time she looked at her son…never to forget?

Why had she sent that letter? Why hadn't she spoken up when

174

she'd had the chance? Now it was too late. Would Andy forgive her if he knew? Avery sighed and tugged the blanket around him, more as a protective gesture than to keep him warm in the late May evening. She brushed a lock of dark hair off his forehead and smiled, still staring but no longer seeing her son's face.

Of course he'd never learn of it. She'd gone to great lengths to make sure. That last letter to Mike was now safely locked away from prying eyes, as was his answer. For some perverse reason, she'd saved both and kept going back to them night after night, as if she needed the reminder to never make the same mistake again. Sometimes she wished the military hadn't been so efficient in sending Mike's belongings back to her.

Her hand went to the heart-shaped locket she wore around her neck. Fingering the sweet gift Mike had sent her, she realized the memento was another reminder. Would she ever be able to take it off and move forward?

A tear broke loose, then trekked down her face. Where had her marriage gone wrong? Why hadn't she been able to love her husband enough for a lifetime? Now that her life was so jaggedly torn apart with his death, why did she wish she could undo what she'd done? *Because your letter most likely caused his death.*

Avery retreated from her son's room.

In the kitchen, Terry stood at the stove and lifted the whistling teakettle. The piercing sound died instantly. No one spoke.

She approached the counter noting two inviting cups and tea bags. "Just what I need."

"You looked a little frazzled." Terry spent a moment pouring hot water over the bags. Once done, she set the teakettle down before handing her the cup. "Figured you could use my calming remedy before I take off."

Avery's lips curled at the edges, forming the genuine smile that wouldn't come earlier. Terry's answer to every problem lay in a cup of tea—that and the accompanying conversation.

"Thanks," she murmured, lifting the cup to her lips. She leaned against the counter Breathing in the aroma of the hot liquid, her smile increased. There might actually be some validity to the thinking, since she *was* feeling better.

"You shouldn't be skulking in cemeteries so close to dark. They aren't safe."

Avery almost choked on her tea. "I was visiting my dead husband's grave, not skulking. Besides, Arlington's an exception." No need to reveal how dangerous her visit had actually been.

The night's events had proven Arlington National Cemetery wasn't the safest place on earth, in fact had become a place to avoid, for now. Being shot at was enough to scare anyone senseless. She was safe and sound in her own kitchen. The danger had long passed. Now that the threat seemed far away, almost a distant memory, the idea somehow paled to the thought of being yanked to the ground by a stranger and then kissing him in a wild moment. A flush of heat streaked up her face. She quickly brought the tea closer to her mouth to camouflage her reaction. She and Terry shared secrets. Her sister even knew of Avery's request for a divorce from her husband, something no one else knew except her lawyer. She couldn't share this. Not yet.

If Terry caught wind of anything happening tonight, Avery would have to relay all the specifics…and quite frankly, she wasn't exactly sure what those specifics entailed. She certainly wouldn't be able to articulate so much as an inkling of what she'd been thinking. All she'd do is upset her sister. She had no idea why someone shot at her or even if she was the target.

Had to be him. As for the other? It was anyone's guess why an unknown man had drawn such a strong response, especially when her husband, whom she'd idolized as a teen and felt the luckiest person in the world to marry, never had. It had to be some kind of awkward response to her situation. Guilt and grief mixed with fear, resulting in an emotional overload.

"You look like you're feeling better. Your color's back." Terry shook her head and tsk-tsked like the older sister she was. "I just wish something more than a cemetery visit had caused it."

Avery's laugh, an indisputable burst of humor absent since

176

before Mike's deployment to Afghanistan four months ago, felt natural. She took another long sip of tea. Then she exhaled, holding on to her smile. Maybe she was analyzing this from the wrong angle. Maybe the emotional overload from her near-death experience had been a good thing because suddenly she felt less encumbered. Freer. Something *had* happened tonight outside of the craziness of stray bullets and kissing strangers. Something inside her had changed, making her think of life beyond guilt.

She sighed. If only that were possible. She had no idea what the future held. All she knew was at that moment she felt…alive.

~

He'd begun tailing Avery Montgomery's car on her way out of the cemetery, following her until a few blocks from her house where he'd turned off and had circled back. He now sat half a block away, watching the house through binoculars.

All was calm. Upstairs, a few lights burned, revealing several open windows. He did a visual of the dark yard and noted a couple of tall trees. One might provide the means to get inside. Due to the earlier incident at the cemetery, tonight wasn't the time to try. She'd be wary and on her guard. He was thankful she hadn't called military police. That would have caused major headaches for all involved.

He rolled his eyes, wondering how this fucking operation had derailed so far off its original track. He didn't like putting innocent civilians at risk but the risk was necessary in this instance, according to his superiors. He started the car and pulled away from the curb.

He'd return at dawn and wait for an opportunity to search her house.

Available in print and e-book format at on-line publishers like Amazon, Barnes & Noble, and Kobo.